The Twins of
FALCONIA

DAVID CARTER

Published in Australia by Sid Harta Books & Print Pty Ltd,
ABN: 34632585293
23 Stirling Crescent, Glen Waverley, Victoria 3150 Australia
Telephone: +61 3 9560 9920, Facsimile: +61 3 9545 1742
E-mail: author@sidharta.com.au

First published in Australia 2021
This edition published 2021
Copyright © David Carter 2021
Cover design, typesetting: WorkingType (www.workingtype.com.au)

Carter, David
The Twins of Falconia
ISBN: 978-1-925707-41-0
pp338

ABOUT THE AUTHOR

David Carter is a retired tax accountant. These days he spends his time buying and selling antiques and collectables and one day he may actually make a profit. He also enjoys playing chess and reading. His favourite author is Bernard Cornwell, but he also enjoys many more historical and other writers.

He lives near the picturesque Port Noarlunga and Christies Beach in Adelaide, South Australia, and is fortunate to live near one of the best wine regions in the world.

This book is dedicated to my granddaughter,

Charlotte Logan, for whom it was written.

I acknowledge the help I received for this book and thank Alison, Charlotte, Judith, Stuart and Yolande. I also thank Luke Harris, my editor Marie Pietersz and Sid Harta Publishers.

Map of Strasia

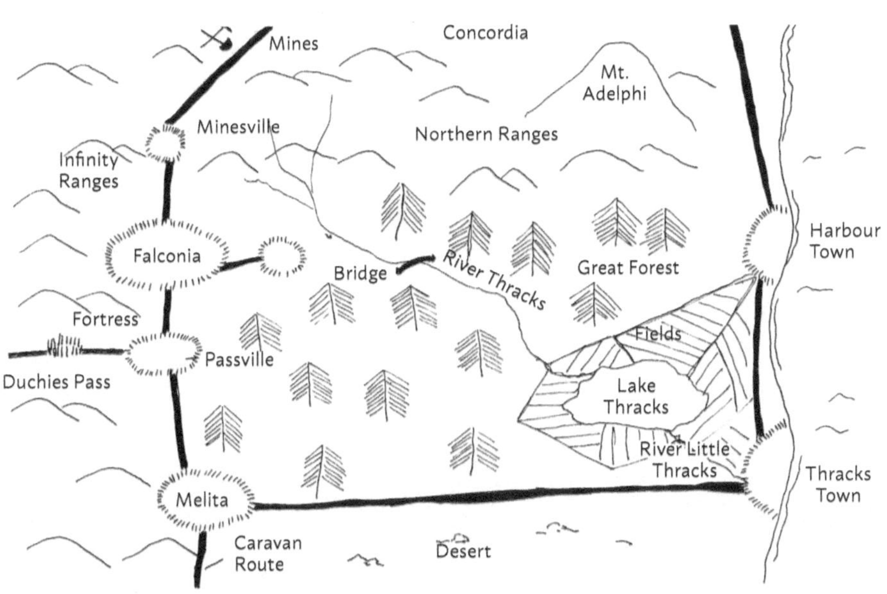

CHAPTER 1

Charlotte screamed. The razor-sharp claw of the massive manticore missed her face by mere inches and she fell backwards to the ground. She stared horrified at the beast that now stood over her and found herself unable to move. She had been picking spring herbs on the outskirts of the great forest, half a mile across the fields from the walls of Harbourtown and now it looked like they would be the last herbs she would ever pick. She looked up at the huge creature which loomed over her, its ugly human face smiling as it licked its lips. 'Now you'll make a pretty little morsel,' it laughed, as it lowered its head with its massive jaws towards Charlotte. Suddenly its head stopped moving. It had looked into Charlotte's blue eyes and frozen.

Neither beast nor girl moved for several seconds; then the stillness was shattered as a trumpet sounded from Harbourtown.

The manticore shook its head, looked at the town and grinned. 'They'll be too late to save you. You are all mine.' It leaned back and raised its lion claw ready to swipe Charlotte's head with the sharp, needle-like points. It screamed with pleasure as it started to slash down with its paw, then screamed again even louder and arched its back as a throwing axe cut deep into its ribs. It had been thrown spinning sideways by a knight in full shining armour, mounted on a jet-black horse. The manticore, with the axe still embedded in its ribs, blood dripping from the wound, shook its six-foot-high lion's body and left Charlotte still lying on the ground unhurt as its human face turned to stare at the knight.

'You will die for that,' the manticore snarled. The knight just laughed, the sound hollow through his fully enclosed helmet. He dismounted carefully from his horse, never taking his eyes off the manticore. 'You stay here, Jenny. That scorpion sting on its tail will kill you.' He lifted his sword and his white shield, which had a red fist emblazed on it, from the straps on his saddle, leaving the large battle-axe behind.

'It will kill you, too,' the manticore spat, as it

approached the knight. Its tail suddenly flicked forward to hit him in the chest. The knight staggered backwards dropping his shield, which he had yet to thread his arm through, and then stopped and laughed. 'This is the best armour in Concordia; you'll blunt your sting.'

The manticore screamed again, 'Then, at least I'll kill the girl.' It turned back to where Charlotte had lain, but she was no longer there. She had seized her chance and was now hiding in the trees watching the battle. 'No ...,' it screamed and turned back to the knight and charged. The knight braced himself for the impact, holding his sword like a spear, but the manticore swerved at the last second and headed towards Jenny. The knight dropped his sword as the beast charged past. He dived at the manticore grabbing for his throwing axe, which was still embedded in the manticore's side.

He succeeded in grabbing the axe, which tore the manticore's side open even more as the axe came loose and stayed in the knight's hand. The manticore once again screamed, then whimpered loudly as it came to a halt, blood pouring from its side. It flicked its sting at the knight yet again, this time hitting the knight's helmet. The knight again staggered back, dropping the axe, and falling to the ground with his helmet flying away leaving his head unprotected. His long blond hair cascaded around his face. The manticore smiled as it now loomed over the knight. 'Nice battle, but now you die. Pity about the girl, though. Maybe next time.' The manticore looked towards Harbourtown as another trumpet sounded and from the open gate soldiers could be seen riding fast. The manticore smiled. 'Too far away. They'll be too late. Goodbye.' The manticore opened its great mouth and dipped its head towards the knight.

Blood started to pour from the manticore's forehead as a horseshoe mark appeared there. The manticore turned its head and a second mark appeared on its nose causing even more bleeding. 'Stupid horse,' it muttered through its blood. The manticore reared and flicked its tail with the scorpion sting at Jenny. It should have hit her, but luckily for Jenny it hit the knight's saddle instead. The knight took his chance and rolled away towards his dropped axe. He picked it up and took careful aim and threw it again. This time the axe embedded itself deep in the manticore's neck causing it to lose even more blood. The manticore, now greatly weakened, fell to its knees sobbing with pain. The knight walked to his sword, stooped and picked it up. He approached the manticore and stood before the sobbing creature and raised his sword hilt to his forehead in salute. He pronounced in a calm voice, 'Base creature, you fought a good fight.' Then with all his strength forced his sword deep into the manticore's eye. It screamed one last time and finally fell dead.

There was the sound of hooves as a dozen soldiers from the castle arrived on the scene. The only armour they wore were open helmets and breast and back plates. They all carried short lances and sword and bucklers. All were dressed in black uniforms except the leader who was an older, handsome, tall and slender man, with long, blonde, wavy hair. He had blue eyes and a broken nose. He was dressed in red and gold. He dismounted and went and stood next to the dead manticore. 'I've never seen a single man kill one of these things before. It is a great achievement.'

The knight, looking around, answered, 'I did have help.' He went and hugged his horse and then stroked the jet-black mane. 'If it were not for Jenny here, I would be dead.' He looked down at his torso. 'And this new, lighter, stronger armour I'm wearing blunted its sting so that it wasn't able to penetrate my saddle. But where's the girl I rescued?'

'Here I am.' Everyone looked around as the girl came out from the trees. She ran to the knight and threw her arms around him. 'Thank you, thank you for saving me.'

'You're quite welcome.' He looked down at the beautiful blonde, blue-eyed girl who was hugging his armour. 'Well, this new, lighter, stronger armour does have one definite disadvantage,' he laughed.

'I think that is the same as the older, heavier, weaker armour,' the man in red and gold said, smiling. 'I am Burger Rowles and I must thank you for saving my goddaughter's life from this monstrosity.' He gestured towards the dead manticore. 'We don't often see such monsters around here as they are illegal.'

'I'm not sure manticores take much notice of the law,' the knight laughed. 'I am Sir Philip Concord and I am travelling on a mission for my uncle, King Regis of Concordia. I am very happy to have been of assistance,' he said, looking down at the girl who was still hugging his armour, 'especially to such a beautiful lady.' He paused and then asked, '... and you are?'

She released his armour and didn't actually curtsy but nodded her head and shoulders, 'I am Charlotte Silver. I own the apothecary in Harbourtown, and I was collecting herbs for medicines when that creature attacked me.' She shivered. 'I thought I was going to die. It was fortunate that you were here to save me.' Charlotte fumbled at the back of her neck unfastening the chain she was wearing. 'Please accept this with my thanks.' She held out a fine, silver chain which held a small, delicate silver rose.

Sir Philip smiled. 'I will wear it until the end of my

days.' He bent down so Charlotte could fasten it around his neck. Fortunately, the chain was quite long, so it fitted him quite well.

Charlotte smiled back. 'My parents made it before they died.'

Sir Philip hesitated, uncertain. 'I'm sorry to hear about your parents. I couldn't possibly accept such a gift.'

'No, please, they would be happy to know it was worn by the man who saved my life, as am I.'

'In that case, it is my great pleasure to wear it.'

Burger Rowles put his arm around his goddaughter and addressed Sir Philip, 'Well, I hope your mission will give you time to at least come and eat with us and to rest yourself and your horse, er ... Jenny.' He looked at Jenny, who was at least two hands taller than any horse he had seen before, with some concern. 'Who isn't magical at all, I hope?'

'The only thing magical about Jenny is her intelligence and bravery,' Sir Philip assured the burger while stroking Jenny's mane. 'She is one of the best horses in Concordia and that is high praise. Yes, I think I will resume my mission tomorrow. My mission is not a secret. I'm off to Falconia to arrange the purchase of some of their iron ore. It is of higher quality than ours and that higher quality ore is needed for this superior quality armour.' He tapped his chest.

Burger Rowles frowned. 'Well, Queen Katerina of Falconia has a somewhat bad reputation. Most think that she is a witch; besides that, she has also built a temple to Braidos, the God of Chaos.' Sir Philip raised his thick eyebrows. Burger Rowles continued, 'but that should not affect a trade deal.' He smiled. 'When you make more of that armour you must remember to sell me some.' He turned to his men and shouted to one of them, 'Constable Watson, get down off your horse and let Charlotte ride back to town.'

'Stop! There is no need.' Sir Philip bent and gave Charlotte a kiss on the cheek. 'She will ride Jenny.' He lifted her onto his saddle and led Jenny and Charlotte, who rode side saddle, towards Harbourtown.

CHAPTER 2

Scarlett was the name of the exceptionally beautiful
daughter of the Queen of Falconia. She was also
extremely evil. As she grew up, she organised a
gang of girls who went around bullying anyone they
could find. If anyone stood up to them, she would arrange
a "chat" with some of the castle guards. As she grew
older, she used to try more interesting things such as
encouraging boys to kiss her and then have them thrown
into the dungeon when they did. As her mother was an
evil witch, she also studied black magic and was slowly
becoming quite adept. Her mother had married her
father just over seventeen years before, and he had died
in mysterious circumstances just before she was born.
All in all, Scarlett was incredibly happy with her life as

a princess, especially as most of the people around her were made miserable by her presence. She was five feet, eight inches tall, had long blonde hair, beautiful blue eyes, a peaches-and-cream complexion and full lips around a mouth that made her look the most beautiful thing in the world when she smiled, which was usually at someone else's misfortune. She lived in an extremely large castle within a walled town. The castle had a deep moat around it in which lived strange creatures that made sure no one went swimming who wanted to live.

Falconia was an extremely rich and prosperous place. The reason for this was because in the north were mountains that had rich mines of diamonds, gold and iron, which had been stolen from the dwarfs over two hundred years before. To the east and southeast was a massive forest where all sorts of strange and magical creatures dwelt; to the west and northwest were more mountains called the Infinity Ranges and, except for a narrow pass to the southwest which led to the Seven Duchies, were impassable. To the south were rolling hills where there were villages of sheep herders and small farms and the town of Passville. Further south was the town of Melita just before the land became a vast, hot desert.

One pleasant spring day a week after the fight with the manticore, when the sun was shining and the birds were singing, Princess Scarlett and some of her cronies were visiting the town that surrounded the castle. They were in the market square as it was market day. There were many stalls selling everything from precious jewels from the mines to feed for chickens. Princess Scarlett and her friends took anything they wanted without paying. None of the merchants dared protest and it was considered by them as just another cost of doing business. The market was quiet as it always was when Princess Scarlett was there, as no one really wanted to take the risk of offending her and thus be thrown into the dungeon by the sword-armed, open-helmed, chain-mail-clad guards wearing sky-blue and grass-green tabards, emblazoned with the Falconian symbol of a black falcon holding the Great Ring of Falconia in its claws, who patrolled the market, or worse. When she and her cronies left, it became much busier.

A knight rode into the square. He was quite tall, five foot eleven-and-three-quarters, with broad shoulders, long blond hair, blue eyes and a pleasant smile on his smooth, tanned face. His armour was bright and shining in the sun. There was a sword, a throwing axe and a battle axe attached to his saddle and a white shield with a red fist emblazoned upon it. His helmet was on the saddle pommel in front of him, which hid his purse that contained some silver and gold which he used to buy provisions. His horse, Jenny, shook her mane happily as she took her rider into the large market square. The knight was Sir Philip Concord and at that moment he had not a care in the world.

He stood up in his stirrups and looked around the thinly populated square and saw Princess Scarlett with three friends. He immediately shouted, 'Charlotte,' and rode quickly towards her. Princess Scarlett looked up and saw him riding towards her. She froze. Jenny stopped just two yards from the Princess, and Sir Philip leapt down from her and rushed up to Princess Scarlett and gave her a huge kiss on the cheek. 'What are you doing here?' he exclaimed. 'I can't believe you are here, especially when I rode straight here and left you behind.'

Princess Scarlett backed away horrified, screaming, 'Guards, guards. Throw this monster into the dungeon immediately. Never let him out.'

She stood there with her friends trying to calm her, but she was shaking as four burly guards grabbed Sir Philip and started to drag him away. He shouted, 'What are you doing? Don't you remember me saving you from the manticore? It's me, Philip!' A guard hit him on the head, and they dragged him to the dungeon, unconscious.

Princess Scarlett, shaken at the audacity of the man

even though clearly a knight, went to find her mother, the queen. The queen was in her private dining room, A bright, well-lit, small square room with large windows and a glass roof and plain cream walls. It had a table with four chairs around it. Queen Katerina was six foot, two inches tall, thin, with long legs, blonde hair, fair skin and cold blue eyes. She always seemed to have a stern look on her face and had an awful, evil-sounding laugh. She was having a late breakfast and didn't really want to be disturbed. She however noted the state of her daughter and told her to sit and tell her what the matter was. Princess Scarlett related to her all that had happened. After she had heard what had happened, she told her daughter to sit down. 'Scarlett,' she uttered, 'I have a story to tell you. You must not interrupt me until I have finished.' Princess Scarlett agreed. 'You have a twin sister called Charlotte.'

Princess Scarlett gasped, 'No!'

'Quiet!' the queen snapped. 'Do not speak until I have finished.' In a calmer voice she continued, 'When you were born almost sixteen years ago you were not alone. There were two of you. You were both born of magic. You are destined to be the most powerful evil witch who has ever lived. But in order to make this happen I had to make a pact with Braidos. One of you would be born evil and the other would be born pure. I had to sacrifice your father to Braidos to make it happen.' Princess Scarlett was turning white as Queen Katerina continued. 'I would have sacrificed your sister also, except Braidos would not let me kill my daughter or arrange for others to harm her. I sent her away. I used to experiment with my magic, creating strange creatures. Some are still alive. The moat monsters are some of them. The others that are left are locked away behind the iron door in my laboratory. I had one with the head of a horse, the body of a man and the legs of a goat. I called him Dobbin. He was told to take her far away and I hoped we would never hear about her ever again. But it seems that this Philip knows her and has even saved her from a manticore.'

Princess Scarlett, forgetting she was not to speak asked, 'What is a manticore?'

The queen answered, 'A manticore is a creature with a human face and head, the body of a lion and a scorpion's tail. If this Philip successfully battled one of them, he must be a very brave and skilled knight. We must speak to him and find out where your sister is.'

'Why?' her daughter asked.

'There is only one person in the world that can prevent you from becoming a great and powerful witch. Guess who?' the queen answered.

Princess Scarlett's hands went to her cheeks. 'Charlotte. But you said that you couldn't cause any harm to come to her.'

'True, as her mother I cannot harm her or cause her to come to any harm. You are not her mother but her sibling and whatever you do is up to you. I think I will have to give you some quick extra lessons.' The queen smiled. 'Of course, you cannot use anything new I show you against your sister.'

Princess Scarlett smiled back. 'Of course not, mother. But why did you name her Charlotte?'

The queen laughed. 'Well, after calling you Scarlett I couldn't be bothered thinking up a good name for something that I thought would die soon, so I just slightly changed your name. I know Charlotte is a dreadful name, but who cares? Now, follow me to my laboratory.'

CHAPTER 3

Sir Philip had been thrown unconscious into a dreadfully deep and damp dungeon of about ten feet by ten feet square and six feet high after having his armour and padded gambeson removed. He was left in just his undergarments. When he regained his senses, he stood. He was just able to stand up straight. His hand went to his neck; the necklace with the rose was gone. He thought that it was probably taken by one of the jailors. The only light entered via a small grille in the door. In the dim light he could make out three other men sitting on the filth-covered floor. Two were in rags and the third wore merchant's clothing. All looked very thin. The merchant got up. He was a short man with dark-brown hair and a dark complexion. 'Welcome, stranger. I am called Nathan; these poor men are Gill and Dwayne.' One of the men in rags raised an arm in acknowledgement and the other had a coughing fit and sank completely to the ground. Nathan looked sadly at the prostrate body. 'I think Gill will die soon if he does not get help.' He turned to Sir Philip, 'and what did you do to join our illustrious company?'

Sir Philip shook his head and answered, 'I kissed someone I thought I knew in the market square and she had me thrown in here.'

'That must have been Princess Scarlett. Was she blonde, so high and with blue eyes?' He raised his hand to just above his head. Sir Philip nodded. 'Yes, that's her.'

'Gill kissed her once and now look at him.' Gill was still coughing quietly while lying on the filthy dungeon floor. 'He thought that she liked him; how wrong can you be?' Nathan shook his head. 'Dwayne was stupid enough to protest when a court judgement was given against him by Queen Katerina even though he was in the right. He was lucky though; many who protest against the queen are thrown to the moat monsters. Myself, I was put in here when I could not pay the new increased Castle Market fee after most of my stock was taken by Princess Scarlett and her gang. Queen Katerina and Princess Scarlett must be two of the evilest people alive. You'll be lucky to get out of here alive.'

Just then the dungeon door was suddenly flung open and two burly jailors entered, dressed entirely in black. One carried a lit torch which burnt with a bright light. The prisoners put their hands to their eyes to protect them. The empty-handed jailor pointed at Sir Philip. 'You! You are to be released and are to see the queen. Quick, move.'

Sir Philip went to leave, but Nathan grabbed his arm. 'Good luck, but don't trust the queen.'

'Silence, scum,' the jailor growled, and hit Nathan on the side of his head. He fell to the ground. Sir Philip ordered, 'Leave him,' and helped Nathan to his feet. The jailor glowered at him. 'I just hope the queen sends you back. Now, hurry! Don't keep the queen waiting.' Sir Philip left the cell followed by the jailors.

Sir Philip was led into a small chamber in which his saddlebags and armour were. There was a washbasin with water and soap for him to use. He took it all in with a quick glance. The jailors went to leave the room. 'Wait, which of you stole my rose necklace?' The two jailors looked at each other but said nothing. 'I will have the queen find it for me.'

One of the jailors scowled and reached into his pouch.

He threw the necklace to the floor. 'I do hope the queen sends you back. I'll really enjoy it.' Sir Philip then checked the rest of his equipment and belongings. He thought that his pouch was lighter than before, but as he hadn't counted his money before entering the town of Falconia he decided to forget the matter. He then washed and pulled out a set of purple doublet and tights. He also wore black boots. He went to fasten the necklace around his neck but hesitated. He didn't have a rational explanation why, but he felt he should not wear it in the queen's presence. He placed it in his pouch. He then left the small chamber and discovered that there was a liveried guard outside it. The guard ordered, 'Follow me.'

He was led into a great entrance hall which had a pair of large, oak doors with iron studs at the end. In the hall was Sir John Amberleigh, the Royal Chamberlain, a small, black-haired, mousey-looking man with beady, darting eyes and the very guards that threw him in the dungeon. The big difference was that now instead of dragging him to the dungeon, they now treated him with deference. They opened the doors and led him into the vast Throne Room. The room was thirty feet high and the ceiling was painted with murals of various vistas of Falconia. The mountains to the north and west, the forest to the east and the rolling hills to the south. The walls were painted white and there were paintings of previous rulers and country scenes. Paintings of Queen Katerina featured prominently. Doors on one side of the room opened out onto a large balcony that overlooked the castle courtyard. At one end of the room was a three-foot dais, the back and sides of which were covered in ruby-red curtains edged in gold. The queen was sitting on her majestic gold, embossed throne in the centre of the dais. Scarlett was sitting on a smaller identical throne at the left-hand edge of the dais. The group stopped about ten feet from the dais. Sir John Amberleigh took an extra step and announced, 'Your Majesty, Sir Philip Concord of Concordia.'

The queen rose, twirling her ermine cloak as she did so. 'Sir Philip, I must apologise. There has been a dreadful mistake.' She suddenly stopped talking and fixed Sir Philip with a long, cold stare. She shook her head with puzzlement and then continued, 'My daughter thought you were attacking her and panicked. Not knowing who you were, you must realise her actions were understandable.'

Sir Philip bowed. 'Gracious queen, I am Sir Philip Concord, a knight of Concordia, the land on the other side of your Northern Ranges and the nephew of King Regis of Concordia. I think I must have mistaken your daughter for someone else. The resemblance is remarkable. I cannot tell the difference.'

The queen waved her hand, 'This is not impossible.' She sat back down on the throne. 'For Princess Scarlett has a twin called Charlotte.' Sir Philip stood there stunned. 'Just after the twins were born Charlotte was kidnapped by a gang of ruffians and we have never seen or had any news of her since. I have really missed her, and I beg of you to tell myself and her sister where she can be found.'

Sir Philip, remembering his conversation with Nathan, was extremely suspicious of the queen's motives. He replied, 'Your Majesty, Charlotte lives a very quiet life. I feel I should take this news to her and bring her back here myself rather than have strangers suddenly appear before her with news of this great happening.'

Princess Scarlett sprang from her throne. 'How dare you!' she screamed. 'You are talking ...'

'Quiet and sit down.' The queen glared at her daughter who returned to her throne. 'I must apologise again for my daughter. I must admit I am rather shocked that you will not tell us the whereabouts of my lost daughter whom I miss tremendously. I can only assure you that all I want is to see her again and hold her in my arms.' The queen gave herself a hug to emphasise her point.

'I will leave immediately to let her know the news, but I

must re-emphasise my position, Your Majesty.' Sir Philip bowed again.

'I must say that I am disappointed. However, as it is rather late, I insist that you spend the night at the palace to recover from your ordeal and we will equip you for your journey so that you may leave in the morning. I have read your letter to me from your uncle, King Regis, regarding a trade agreement between us for Falconian iron ore in return for Concordian beef. I think it is a perfect trade. Nevertheless, I must emphasise the agreement completely depends upon the result of finding my daughter. Do you understand?'

Sir Philip nodded. 'Yes, Your Majesty.'

'Good. Guards, show him to one of the visitor rooms.' She waved her hand in dismissal. Sir Philip bowed as he, Sir John Amberleigh and the guards left the Throne Room.

Princess Scarlett rose and approached the queen. 'Why not just torture the information out of him?' she demanded.

'I cannot,' the queen replied. 'To do that I would be acting to harm my daughter and it would mean war between Falconia and Concordia, and Concordia has the best fighters on the continent plus minor magicians of its own, and we are not yet ready to beat them. Besides, I am partial to a good steak.' She gave a rare smile. 'On a completely different topic, I have shown you how to conjure a wraith, the wispy smoke creature that is extremely hard to see, haven't I?'

'Yes, mother.'

'Come with me and I will show you how to mix a draught that when you blend it with water will allow a wraith to make an invisible trail to follow whatever creature you get to drink it. It doesn't work on humans, but it does on animals such as horses.'

'I think I would like to learn that very much, mother.'

'Good, but first' — she raised her voice — 'send for the Captain of the Guard.'

Shortly, a tall man in Falconian livery, but with gold epaulettes, entered the room. He had gold, flowing hair, hard brown eyes and a stony face. He bowed. 'Captain Miland at your service, Your Majesty.'

The queen stood. 'Tomorrow morning a knight will be riding out from the castle. I want two of your best men to follow him and report back where he goes.'

Captain Miland bowed again. 'Certainly, Your Majesty. I will arrange it at once. Is that all?'

Queen Katerina waved him away. 'Yes, now go.'

The captain bowed and left. Princess Scarlett looked puzzled. 'Mother, if a wraith is going to trail Sir Philip, and his horse can be easily tracked, why do we need two guards to follow him?'

The queen frowned. 'We must assume that Sir Philip is a clever and cautious man. Remember, he was entrusted with an important mission for his king. He will expect to be followed. If he is not, he will become extremely suspicious. This way he'll spot the guards and lose them, not realising that there is a much better tracker following him as well.'

Princess Scarlett looked at her mother in awe. 'That's brilliant!'

The queen nodded. 'It is, isn't it? Now come, we have lots to do before morning.'

The queen rose and led the way out through the curtains at the back of the dais to go to her laboratory.

CHAPTER 4

The following morning Sir Philip was back in his armour. He made sure that the rose necklace around his neck was inside his breastplate and not showing. After making sure that Jenny had been well looked after the previous night, he saddled her in the main castle stable and checked his equipment to make sure it was all there. The queen had provided a heavy purse of coins which he tied to his belt. He put his purse from Concordia into one of his saddle bags. He was also provided with several days' supply of food and water. He noticed that Jenny seemed a bit skittish and he assumed that was because the guards had stabled her the previous day rather than himself. He then led Jenny into the large castle courtyard. The queen and her daughter entered the castle courtyard from different doors. Princess Scarlett approached the queen. 'Everything is prepared ...'

'Quiet! Do not speak,' the queen snapped, and then she went up to Sir Philip. 'I wish you a safe and speedy journey. You do not know how much I am looking forward to the success of your mission and seeing my daughter again. Tell her I miss her terribly. Her sister does also. We have provided you with some additional gold and silver so that you will not lose out by making this extra journey. She then emphasised, 'and do not forget, the success of this mission guarantees the success of your mission for your uncle, King Regis.'

Princess Scarlett nodded in agreement. Sir Philip bowed and climbed up onto Jenny. 'I will return in about two to two-and-a-half weeks, Your Majesty.' He then rode Jenny out of the main castle gate.

The queen turned to her daughter and told her, 'I hope you have learnt your lessons well. You may have full access to my library for your studies. I do not wish to see you for two weeks. Go!'

Princess Scarlett answered, 'Yes, mother.'

Queen Katerina left the courtyard followed by two guards.

Scarlett watched her leave and whispered to herself, 'I have learnt my lessons extremely well. Bye, bye, sister.'

Sir Philip left the town of Falconia via the main gate on the south of the town. Three pairs of eyes watched him ride through the gate. Captain Gill Miland spoke to his two men who were both mounted on good steeds and wearing smart but inexpensive merchant clothing. 'Remember you are to make sure he arrives safely at his destination and report where that is in the fastest possible way. Don't lose him.' The senior of his two men answered, 'We'll stick like leeches.'

The captain replied, 'Not too close. Don't let him spot you.' Both men saluted by placing their fists over their hearts. The captain continued, 'And don't forget you're merchants, not soldiers.' Both men gave sheepish smiles and then rode out after Sir Philip. The captain mumbled after them, 'Good luck. I think you'll need it.'

The road south was a busy one. There was just the one main road leading from the town of Falconia to the rest of the continent, though there were smaller roads leading to various settlements around the capital. There were several small villages and two towns on the main road south, before it turned east towards Thrackstown on the east coast. The first town was Passville, so called because it was at the turnoff to the only pass in the mountains called Duchies Pass. The pass led to the seven Duchies in the west. It also supplied the fortress at the Falconian end of the pass. The second town was the free town of Melita, named after the wife of the first King of Falconia. She had been born there and the town changed its name to honour the marriage. This was where the road turned east. It was best known as the start of the only known caravan route south across the desert which started fifty miles south of the town. The mountains continued to the west for many more miles and south along the edge of the desert. To the east all along the road from Falconia to about twenty miles just before Melita was the Great Forest. The edge of the forest ranged from a couple of hundred yards to several miles from the road. The furthest distance the forest was away from the road was about twenty-six miles from the capital. To the east the forest crossed the rest of this part of the continent of Strasia to just a few miles from the east coast. The only exception to this were the massive farmlands around Lake Thracks. The land south of the town of Falconia was mainly rolling grassy hills, which were used mainly for sheep and goat farming.

❧

Sir Philip had been planning to travel at a brisk trot and camp out at night, not stopping at any of the villages or towns on his route. He hadn't stopped at any on his way to Falconia from Harbourtown either, being keen to get back to see Charlotte. However, as Jenny was extremely skittish, he travelled at a much slower trot. He still assumed that it was because Jenny had been seen to by Castle Falconia grooms the night before and not himself. He did not know that the princess had prepared a potion during the night which had been added to Jenny's morning bucket of water. It caused Jenny to leave an invisible trail which could only be followed by a wraith. The wraith itself was sticking to the protection of the trees of the Great Forest. Most of the time it could see Sir Philip and Jenny across the grassy hills; when it couldn't, it could sense Jenny. The potion had the added effect of making Jenny skittish.

As he rode south, he greeted all the travellers and merchant caravans that were travelling towards Falconia and those few merchant caravans he overtook going the other way. Several travellers moving at a fast trot or canter overtook him. He did notice a couple of travellers who seemed to be travelling at exactly the same speed as himself. When he had confirmed this after seeing them several times, he patted Jenny's mane and told her, 'Well, it seems the queen doesn't trust us, Jenny.' He continued, 'Well, I hoped we'd be a decent distance beyond Passville tonight and camp out. I think though we'll stop there, and I'll give you a good brush down at an inn. We may feel better tomorrow.'

Shortly after, the wooden walls of Passville came into sight. He rode through the open gate. The pair of guards in Falconian livery and both holding halberds nodded to him as he passed. The gate would be closed at dusk. No one who lived near the Great Forest didn't barricade themselves in at night. One of the first buildings he spotted after the especially functional-looking, gate-guard post was an inn. It was larger than most having three storeys and was painted in the very distinctive black-and-white that most inns were decorated in. There was a swinging inn sign over the front door showing a sleeping man on a wagon and underneath were the words 'The Merchant's Rest'. He rode Jenny into the very large stable behind the inn. It was obviously used by merchants for both their steeds and pack horses. There were already several horses stabled there and a groom, probably hired by the inn offered to rub Jenny down and stable her. Sir Philip declined and rubbed Jenny down himself after removing his saddle, saddle bags and weapons. He then stabled her making sure that she had some of the best grain the groom could supply and a full bucket of water. When he had finished, he tipped the groom a silver coin and ordered him to let him know immediately if Jenny had any problems during the night. He then picked up all his belongings and, staggering under the weight of them, entered the back door of the inn.

CHAPTER 5

Sir Philip entered the tap room of the inn. It was a large square room with a long bar on one side, which ran for most of that side. A pair of doors completed the wall. On the opposite wall was a large fireplace with two large piles of logs on either side. There was a small fire burning even though it was late afternoon on a pleasant, early spring day. The temperature was still warm enough not to need it burning fiercely yet. Sir Philip thought to himself that this was one of the advantages of a more southern spot in the spring. Back at Concord Castle, the Concordian Capital, snow would still be on the ground. On the wall in front of him were double front doors and two large bay windows. Burning oil lamps were hanging from the ceiling. The many tables were mainly unoccupied at this time of day, with just a few merchants, who like himself had decided not to push on and camp, but instead take the more pleasant option of a soft bed for the night. Behind the bar was a short, balding, middle-aged, extremely well-muscled man with a broken nose and bushy eyebrows. There were also two pretty serving girls in green dresses and white aprons. Sir Philip assumed the man was the proprietor and walked to the bar clunkily carrying his saddle and weapons with him. He dropped them on the bar and the balding man smiled. 'Looks like you've got quite a load there. Would you like a room?'

Sir Philip answered, 'Yes, please, just for tonight. I've already stabled my horse.'

'Key or no key?' the innkeeper asked.

'Key or no key?' Sir Philip repeated, puzzled.

The innkeeper smiled again. 'Key or no key? Would you like a room with a lock, or are you willing to take your chances?'

'Ah, a lock, please. Could I also purchase a hot meal, breakfast and some extra corn and oats for my horse?' Sir Philip stopped and mused for a moment. 'Oh, and some ale.'

The innkeeper nodded. 'Certainly! The hot food won't be ready for about an hour or so, but you can have some bread and cheese while you're waiting.' He turned to a drawer behind the bar and took a key from it. 'Number five on the first floor.' He banged on the wall behind the bar. 'Johnathon will show you the way and help you carry your equipment. My name is Claude.'

He stuck out his hand and Sir Philip took it. 'I'm Philip Concade. I'm from Concordia and I'm on my way back.' He decided not to use his real name to confuse anyone following him.

'Well, Phil ...'

Sir Philip inwardly cringed.

'That'll be five Falconian Silvers.'

Sir Philip's eyebrows raised. Falconian coins were the largest on the continent, followed by those of Concordia and then the three free towns, Melita, Thrackstown and Harbourtown. The large mix of coins from the Seven Duchies were the smallest.

'Well, you're lucky, we'll be much busier later when more merchants arrive. Rooms at this time of year are at a premium.' He turned and banged the wall again. 'Where is that lazy boy?'

The "boy" Johnathon, a tall, lanky youth of about twenty, which made him older than Sir Philip, came out of the closed door. Claude ordered him, 'Help Phil here to room five.' Sir Philip finished counting out five silvers from the pouch the queen had given him — she had been very generous — and followed Johnathon through the second door. 'I'll have some bread, cheese and ale waiting for you when you come back down,' he called after their retreating backs.

About fifteen minutes later, Sir Philip returned to the tap room, where there were a few more people, mainly merchants. He was once again wearing his purple doublet, purple tights and boots. He lamented that his saddlebags didn't have a lot of space for spare clothes. He also wore at his waist a slender double-edged dagger. Claude shouted to him, 'Hi, Phil, there's some bread and cheese on that table near the back door for you and a mug of ale.' Sir Philip winced inwardly again, nodded his thanks and went to consume his pre-dinner repast. He ate and drank slowly while studying the people in the room. He made wagers with himself on which were the two men following him. He finally decided on two large burly men near the front door. A singer with a mandolin came in. He was tall, fair and handsome, dressed entirely in green. He went and sat near the fire and started to tune his instrument. Claude waved to him and then announced in a loud voice to the entire room, 'Those having a hot meal, hot lamb and vegetable stew and potatoes in fifteen minutes.'

Sir Philip decided to check on Jenny before eating. He went out the back door and through the yard to the stables. Jenny was still in her stall munching happily on a half trough of oats. He rubbed Jenny's ears, 'Eaten most of it already, girl.' The water bucket was three-quarters full. 'Well, you look set up for the night. See you early tomorrow.' He walked back through the yard. There were two men in the yard, both making use of the back wall. Sir Philip noted that one of them was one of the two men he guessed was following him. He re-entered the tap room to find that three large merchants were sitting at his table.

Claude was walking towards the table with a tray holding a steaming bowl of lamb stew and a mug of beer. He addressed the men, 'Excuse me, sirs, but that table belongs to Phil here.'

The biggest of the three, a well-dressed, bald, giant of a man, about six-feet-four, with a scar on his left cheek, laughed. 'Well, we're here now.' He looked at Sir Philip and noted the silver chain and rose. 'That fop can go sit in the corner.'

'But, sirs,' Claude began.

Sir Philip held up his hand. 'No, that's alright, Claude. I'll sit in the corner. I just want a quiet evening.'

'That's one way of saying, I'm just scared,' the giant added, with a sneer.

Claude, remembering the weapons and armour that Sir Philip had arrived with, was glad that there wasn't going to be trouble in his inn. He said to Sir Philip, 'Thanks, Phil, I'll get you an extra mug of ale and some lemon pie, on the house.'

'Maybe you should kiss him too and tuck him in afterwards,' the large merchant laughed maliciously.

Both Sir Philip and Claude ignored him. Claude set the tray down on the empty table in the corner and Sir Philip sat and started to eat. As Claude walked back to the bar, the merchant shouted to him, 'Six ales, three stews and three pies, quickly.'

Claude shouted back. 'You'll be served in your turn, sirs.' The three men didn't look happy.

Meanwhile, more customers, a lot of them local, had entered the inn, obviously to listen to the singer, who was quite talented. Sir Philip found himself tapping his foot and clapping along to the music along with most of the people in the room.

'You, stupid, clumsy fool!' One of the waitresses had slipped and spilt some ale on the large merchant. 'These clothes cost a fortune.'

'I'm very sorry, sir,' the waitress, who was about sixteen and attractive, whispered with tears in her eyes, quite distressed.

'That's not good enough.' He looked her up and down and then grabbed her. The tray she was carrying was taken by one of the other men at the table. 'I'm going to horsewhip you, you clumsy fool.'

The waitress started to struggle and gave a little scream. Claude appeared holding a short cudgel and the room went quiet. 'Let her go.'

'She just ruined my doublet. I should be allowed to punish her for the damage she did,' the merchant answered, still holding the girl.

Claude held the merchant's eyes. 'You heard her, she apologised. No one, I repeat no one, threatens any of my people. Now, let her go!' Claude finished his statement with a raised voice.

'We've already paid your exorbitant price for a locked room. We've paid for our food. She's ruined my doublet. I should be allowed to punish her, and I will.' He held the girl tighter.

'I repeat, let her go.' While the two were arguing, the merchant, who had taken the tray, also extremely well-built, but not as tall as the speaker, had put the tray down and worked his way behind Claude. The third large merchant had joined the first and was now also holding the girl. The merchant behind Claude pulled out a knife and held it at Claude's back. 'I'd drop the cudgel if I were you and let us take the girl.'

Suddenly he screamed as a knife slashed into his right wrist, fortunately for him, missing his artery. He dropped the knife as blood started to gush from the wound. Sir Philip moved away from the merchant, still with his dripping dagger in his hand, to Claude's side. 'Someone help him stop the bleeding,' he asked the room at large, without taking his eyes from the largest merchant. 'You were asked to let her go.'

The merchant answered, 'I'm going to chop you into little pieces, you little fop.' He let go of the girl, leaving her in his companion's hands. He pulled out the knife he was wearing at his belt and took his companion's knife so that he had one in each hand.

While this was happening, several of the locals had stood and grouped together behind Claude. Claude looked around. 'You going to take all of us?'

The merchant looked at the large group of men, smiled and shrugged. 'Another time, fop.' He turned to the man still holding the girl. 'Let her go.' He did so. 'Well, after we stop James' bleeding, we'll go to bed.'

Claude scowled, 'Not here, you won't. I'll have your stuff thrown into the street and you can pick it up. I'll have your horses taken out there as well.'

'But we've already paid,' the large merchant protested.

'Take it up with the mayor. I will if you don't get out right now.' Claude answered.

The two men scowled as they helped their friend, who had a tightly bound wrist thanks to two other merchants in the room, out of the front door. Most of the customers jeered them on their way. Claude turned to Sir Philip. 'Thanks, Phil, another ale on the house?'

'No, thank you, I have an early start tomorrow. I think I'll head to my room. Do you keep copies of the door keys?'

'All innkeepers do, in case they're needed. Don't worry, they're locked away safely with only one key.' He patted a bunch of keys at his waist. 'Which reminds me,' he looked around and saw Johnathon behind the bar. 'Johnathon, get Locky, and the two of you get their horses out of the stable and tie them round the front. I'll get their bags.' He turned to Sir Philip. 'I hope you have a good night.'

Sir Philip answered, 'I hope so, also,' and turned to leave the room, only to bump into the waitress he had helped rescue. She looked up at him with puppy-dog eyes.

'I just wished to thank you for your help in rescuing me, I won't forget what you did.' She looked down, blushing.

I'm going to have to stop rescuing maids in distress, Sir Philip thought. 'My pleasure, I'm just glad you weren't hurt. I hope we meet again.' He gave her a quick kiss on the cheek and quickly walked to the door which led to the stairs.

CHAPTER 6

That same evening Queen Katerina left her laboratory at an extremely late hour. She had used a shimmering charm on herself so that anyone who looked at her would not see her. She exited the castle through a secret passage that led under the moat and terminated inside a derelict building on the edge of the square on which the Temple of Braidos was built. The temple was a large, black building which had eight columns holding the tall, triangular roof. Stairs led to a narrow patio along the front of the building. Two large, black iron doors stood open. No one saw her enter the temple or her progress towards the altar where a figure knelt wearing a black habit and cowl. The queen glanced around at the large temple as she approached the figure. A pale glow emanated from the high, gothic ceiling which lit the temple. There was a complete lack of any furniture on the deep-red, wall-to-wall carpet except for the altar, which was covered with black cloth. The front of the cloth showed a blood-red star inside a shimmering purple circle. On the altar was a large, golden chalice and nothing else. The queen halted before she reached the kneeling figure. 'Roget, I wish to speak to Braidos.'

Roget rose and turned to face the queen. He gave a slight bow, his features hidden inside the cowl. 'I will see if the great one wishes to be summoned.'

He raised a skeletal hand and gestured at the two iron doors, which slammed shut. He then turned towards the altar and approached it. As he approached, he intoned words very softly. The queen strained to hear them, but even though she had magically enhanced her hearing, she could not make them out. He lifted the large, golden chalice and drank from it, then returned it to the altar. Nothing happened. They stood silently for almost three minutes, waiting. There was a sound like a thunderclap and the temple darkened. A black whirlwind started to grow above the altar. In the centre of the whirlwind a large dark figure started to appear. The dark figure slowly continued to form from the top of the head down. It looked like a male. He was bald with scarlet-coloured skin that glowed. The eyes were jet-black, the nose little more than a slit and the lips a deep blood-red. The cloak on his bare back was as black as his eyes. He looked extremely muscular. His legs were not seen if they existed, as the whirlwind still swirled below his waist. He lifted one long, thin arm and pointed a long, slim finger at the queen. 'Why have you requested my presence?'

'Braidos, I need to speak to you about my daughters,' the queen replied.

Braidos smiled. 'Daughters? Not daughter?'

'You must know Charlotte still lives,' the queen snapped.

'True. But you did not. How did you learn?'

'A knight mistook Scarlett for her. He kissed her in the square.'

Braidos chuckled. 'That must have given her a slight surprise. So, what do you want?'

Queen Katerina stared icily at Braidos, 'Charlotte dead and Scarlett the only heir to the throne.'

'You would condemn your own daughter?'

'I never wanted twins. This is just your warped sense of humour. There should have only been Scarlett,' the queen replied, coldly.

Braidos rose further into the air. 'Careful of what you say to me. I still hold your fate in my hands.' He spread his hands. 'I am the God of Chaos, if everything was ordered and expected, what use would I be?'

The queen clenched her fists. 'But ...'

Braidos clapped his hands together to the sound of thunder. 'Cease this complaining. Did I not supply you with the two vials, one for you and one for the king that ensured you became pregnant? Did I not supply you with the vial that ensured the king died from "natural" causes? Did you not promise that you would do nothing to harm your child?' He gave a little chuckle. 'Or, as it has turned out, children. The answer to all these questions is, yes. Is it my fault you entrusted one child to a creature that you created? Probably too well as it kept her alive. You have no cause to complain.'

The queen stamped her foot. 'You told me my daughter would be the start of a great lineage.'

'In Chaos, nothing is certain, but the chances are good.' Braidos shook his head. 'I grow tired of this conversation. Be careful of what you do. I will be watching.' There was another thunderclap as Braidos once again clapped his hands and he shrank back into the whirlwind which then faded until it disappeared altogether.

The queen turned and glared at Roget. Roget gave a slight bow and gestured at the doors, which opened. 'Your Majesty,' he intoned. The queen strode quickly towards the doors renewing the shimmering charm as she did so.

No one saw her re-enter the castle.

CHAPTER 7

Sir Philip rose long before dawn the next day reasoning that he should be able get a good head start on the men following him. After he had donned his armour and grabbed his saddle together with his weapons, he crept down the stairs as silently as he could which, together with a couple of squeaky steps and his metal armour, was not that quiet. He entered the tap room and saw one of the men who was following him asleep with his head in his arms at the table by the back door that he had briefly occupied the previous night. Sir Philip headed for the back door and beyond that the stables. He reached the back door, which was bolted and had a metal bar across it to make it secure. He lifted the bar and placed it silently next to the door. He then tried to pull back the bolt. It was stuck. He hit the bolt with his gauntlet and it slid back with a loud crack. The man at the table jumped up with a start. For a second, both the man and Sir Philip stared into each other's eyes. They both muttered expletives and then burst into action. The man ran towards the door that led to the bedrooms while Sir Philip ran for the stable.

Jenny whinnied happily when she saw Sir Philip and Sir Philip took the time to give her a quick hug. 'Sorry, girl, we're in a great hurry. We have to move fast.' He quickly saddled Jenny and mounted. As he rode out of the stable his two shadows ran into it to get their own horses. In the courtyard, Locky was walking to the stable. Sir Philip threw him a silver coin. 'Quick, Locky, open the gate and then close it after me, then hide.' Locky looked at the coin in his hand and then ran to the courtyard gate. As soon as the gap was large enough Sir Philip and Jenny rode through and Locky immediately started to close it.

Sir Philip rode to the South Gate of Passville, which was just opening with the dawn, and rode out on the road to Melita. 'We'll outride them easily enough,' he told Jenny, with a smile, 'then we'll bypass Melita and just keep going. They'll never catch us, girl.'

Unfortunately for Sir Philip, Jenny was still skittish and after a couple of miles he realised that he was not going to outride his shadows and that it would not be too long before they caught up. The Great Forest was, at this point, only half a mile to his left. 'Let's go hide in the forest,' he muttered to Jenny.

He rode to the edge of the forest and entered the trees. About ten minutes later, his two shadows rode past at a fast canter. He watched them until they were out of sight over a crest. 'Well, they're now ahead of us. Looks like we'll have to go through the forest. Let's see if we can find a trail.' He turned Jenny and rode further into the trees. He did not see a wispy figure hiding in the trees to his left which floated after them.

As he travelled further into the forest, it became darker and the trees more misshapen and gnarled. The tracks were narrower and he was thankful for his knight training, which included woodcraft and learning how to determine his travelling direction from the sun and the moss on trees. Fortunately, Jenny had an amazing sense of direction, which also helped. Sir Philip had found an animal track heading on a westerly course and followed it until it turned south. He then dismounted and chopped through the undergrowth with his throwing axe in a more north-westerly direction. He eventually came across a more well-trodden track heading in the right way and remounted Jenny. 'I hope we don't meet anything too large along here. It's a bit cramped for a fight,' he told Jenny.

They did encounter a large wolf heading the other way but, fortunately, it decided that the armoured knight and horse could be tough opponents and turned and loped away. Just before dusk, he found a small clearing next to a stream. 'At least you've got grass and water,' he told Jenny, as he brushed her down before resaddling. 'I need to keep you saddled though in case of an emergency. This forest hasn't got a good reputation.' He then built a fire and cooked some lamb which he had been supplied by the castle and settled down still in his armour to what was an uneventful night.

The following day, after spending a morning following small tracks heading in the right general direction, Sir Philip heard a faint constant noise. As they rode on, it became louder and louder until the roaring drowned every other noise in the forest. Then, suddenly, there were no more trees. In front of them was a ten-foot-wide ditch which contained a wild, fast, rocky river. The rapids were the worst he had ever seen. This was the River Thracks, the largest on the continent. It ran from the mountains in the north all the way into Lake Thracks which lay between Harbourtown and Thrackstown. Thrackstown so called because the river Little Thracks ran out of the lake and through the town. The land around the lake was the major food bowl for the entire continent of Strasia. Sir Philip looked at the water as it crashed fiercely into the many rocks and boulders in the rapids. He patted Jenny's head. 'Well, I don't think we'll be crossing here. Let's check up river,' he shouted into her ear. 'At least that's almost the right direction.'

He followed the riverbank upstream along a narrow, animal track which ran between the forest and the river. After about two miles, the river was still a raging torrent hurling itself against the rocks. 'Surely, this can't go on much more,' he shouted to Jenny, as the noise the river was making got even louder.

Then there it was. A bridge! The strangest looking bridge he had ever seen. It looked as if a giant spider had woven it. It was very narrow, had a single arch and only a low balustrade. It was like a strange cobweb of silk. He approached the bridge. 'Jenny, you wait here,' he shouted. 'Let's see if it will hold my weight.'

He dismounted and walked towards the bridge. As he got closer it seemed that he was trying to wade through treacle. The sound of the river also lessened. When he was only four feet away from the bridge, he was unable to move any closer and all sound from the river had disappeared. At the base of the bridge the air began to shimmer, and several small creatures slowly appeared. They were about six inches tall and were brightly clothed. They looked beautifully human except that they all had thin gossamer wings. They looked up at Sir Philip and he could see them conferring. One, a female dressed in red and having blonde hair, flew up and hovered about two feet from his face. From this distance he could see that she had incredibly pale skin, pointy ears and green eyes. He immediately thought, *A fairy, but they're not real!* while staring at the stunning being.

She spoke with a voice that rang like a bell, 'Why are you and your companion here at our bridge?'

Sir Philip gave what he assumed was his most winning smile. 'My lady.' He believed this was a safe form of address. 'We wish to …'

The fairy had flown up so that he now had to look up to her and her eyes flashed with anger. 'I am a queen! You will address me as Your Majesty!'

'I'm very sorry, Your Majesty,' he said quickly, while trying to bow. He still couldn't move. 'My companion and I are trying to find a way across the rapids. We will gladly pay for the privilege of doing so.'

The queen looked at him intently. 'There is something strange about you that I cannot place.' She looked around at the forest behind him. 'And there is a trace of something evil in the forest. I do not like this.' She looked back at Sir Philip. 'What will you give me?'

Sir Philip had the pouch the queen had given him tied to his belt. His pouch was in his saddle bag. He thought about offering a silver piece for passage but decided to play safe. 'I will give you a gold piece, Your Majesty.'

The queen smiled and flew back down to be level with his face. 'Gold? Most people just offer silver. It buys a pass.' She hesitated. 'Payment first, of course.'

Sir Philip smiled back; he found he now could move. He removed his gauntlets and placed them on the ground. He opened the pouch that Queen Katerina had given him and picked out a gold piece, which he handed to the queen with a bow. The queen took the coin, looked at it and screamed. 'The evil queen.' She turned and threw the coin into the rapids. Sir Philip found that he could not move yet again.

'I have other coins, Your Majesty. Please let me get them.' Philip declared, urgently.

The queen had flown back up to where she had been before. 'You have displeased me greatly, but we have made a bargain. I will see your other coin.'

Able to move again, he turned and called Jenny. Jenny walked up to him and he took a Concordian gold piece from his pouch in the saddle bag, bowed and handed it to the queen. The queen looked at the Concordian coin with its portrait of King Regis. 'This is satisfactory, it will buy a pass.'

He turned to Jenny. 'Okay, you go first.' Jenny moved to the bridge, took a tentative first step and then gently crossed the bridge to the other side of the rapids. Once across, she turned and looked to Sir Philip to follow. Sir Philip called, 'Good girl,' and went to follow, only to find that once again he couldn't move. He looked at the queen who was still a couple of feet from his face. 'What's happening?'

The queen, who had somehow disposed of the coin in her hands while he was watching Jenny, gave an evil grin. 'Your companion has paid to cross our bridge. You have yet to pay.'

'I've already given you a Concordian gold piece. What trickery is this,' Sir Philip shouted.

'One coin, one pass,' the queen smirked. 'One of you has already passed. You need to now pay for your pass.'

Sir Philip shook his head. 'I see, extortion; and I took you at your word.'

The queen's eyes flashed angrily. 'I never said your coin would buy more than one pass. It bought a pass. One of you has taken it, now the other must pay for theirs.'

Sir Philip raised his hands in a placating gesture.

'Okay, let me get my saddlebag and I will give you another gold coin.'

The queen, still smirking, said, 'You may not cross the river before payment. You must ask your companion to give me the coin for your payment.'

Sir Philip shook his head with exasperation. 'And just how is Jenny to do that?' The queen shrugged. He continued, 'I know, why don't you just fly over there and get a coin out of the saddle bag.'

'We are not allowed to take our payment; it must be given,' the queen answered, crossing her arms.

Sir Philip slumped, then raised his head. He was still wearing his helmet. 'I will give you my helmet. It's worth at least a gold piece, probably a lot more.'

The queen flew above him again and screamed, 'You would offer a fairy, iron?'

Sir Philip muttered an expletive to himself, while thinking, *Iron kills fairies. Bad move.* He said out loud, 'Sorry, Your Majesty, I wasn't thinking. What do you suggest I should do?' hoping that the queen would be reasonable.

The queen scratched her chin. 'I suggest you follow the river upstream for about fifty miles until you pass the rapids. Be careful when you climb the three sets of cliffs. It could be hard in your armour. Your companion will probably have to wait for you to come back on the other side at the base of the first cliffs.' She smiled gracefully. 'I hope that helps.'

Sir Philip had never felt so helpless before. Not even when he was in the Falconian jail. There at least he may have been able to get a message to his uncle, the king. Here, he had to travel a hundred miles on foot through sometimes almost impenetrable forest, navigate six set of cliffs and face who knew what sort of creatures. At least his armour was lighter than normal, but he felt despair. He would fail his mission for the king. He would fail to warn Charlotte about Queen Katerina. Charlotte! He had Charlotte's silver rose and chain.

He looked at the queen. 'I do have something of value, but its value to me is greater than its monetary worth. I would make a bargain. I will give it to you as collateral for my crossing the river to Jenny, and once across I will give you five Concordian gold pieces for it back.'

The queen tilted her head. 'Five gold pieces. It must be something of great value. Show it to me and then I will decide.'

'I need to take off my helmet.' He found he had more movement, but it was still very sluggish. 'It was given to me by a lady I am coming to find I am exceedingly fond of, if not love.' He placed his helmet on the ground next to his gloves. He lifted the chain from around his neck and held it out allowing the rose pendant to swing.

The queen looked aghast. She turned and flew down to her companions and seemed to have an urgent conversation with them. A male fairy in blue attire flew up from the group. He was older, greying and distinguished. He was holding the gold coin Sir Philip had paid earlier. He bowed to Sir Philip. 'My name is Aengus. I am the chief advisor to Queen Lumina, and you are?'

Sir Philip, now able to move, bowed. 'I am Sir Philip Concord, nephew of King Regis of Concordia.'

Aengus looked at the silver rose. 'How came you by that?'

'I saved its owner from a manticore. She gave it to me as a token of thanks. I've promised never to part with it.'

'Do you know what it is?'

Sir Philip looked puzzled. 'A silver rose?'

Aengus smiled. 'It is a minor charm of power. It helps to protect.'

'It didn't save its owner from the manticore.'

'As I said, its power is minor, but the manticore didn't kill her, did it?'

Sir Philip looked thoughtful. 'No.'

Aengus smiling continued, 'And it's going to get you across our bridge. What's more amazing is it even gets you an apology from the queen and your coin back.' He held out the coin to Sir Philip.

Sir Philip shook his head. 'No, thank you, let the queen keep it as a souvenir. It may make her kinder to other travellers.'

Aengus, still smiling, whispered, 'I wouldn't bet on that.' Louder, he added, 'Please make use of our bridge whenever you wish.' He waved his arms invitingly towards the bridge.

Sir Philip, noting that the other fairies had disappeared, answered, 'Thank you.' He put the silver chain and rose back around his neck and then picked up his helmet and gauntlets and started towards the bridge.

Aengus shouted to him, 'The queen was right about one thing.' Sir Philip hesitated. 'There is a trace of something evil in the forest. Be careful.'

'I will,' Sir Philip answered and then strode quickly across the bridge. He remounted Jenny and patted her neck. 'I'm going to be very glad when we're finally out of this forest.' They started to ride away from the bridge.

Once again, he did not see the wispy figure that floated across the rapids thirty yards downstream.

CHAPTER 8

The same day that Sir Philip encountered the fairies, the queen in all her royal finery was holding court. She was receiving reports from the Ambassador of Mayflor, a tall, good-looking man wearing a scarlet robe. Mayflor was one of the seven duchies that existed beyond the Duchies Pass in the western mountains. The ambassador was actually her second cousin and blond like all the queen's blood relatives. Queen Katerina was originally from there and the Duke and Duchess of Mayflor were her parents. Most of the report was greetings from her parents and information of how her many relatives were getting on. While this was happening, a tall, dark-haired man strode into the Throne Room. He was well dressed in green and brown and wore a brown cloak. His face was rugged and there was a scar which ran from his milky left eye down his cheek to his chin. His left hand was missing, in its place a shining, steel hook. Everyone stopped what they were doing as he entered, the report forgotten. He ignored everyone in the room until he was standing before the throne, where he bowed and spoke to the queen, 'Urgent news, Your Majesty.'

The queen looked down at him with some disdain, 'You are always so dramatic, Sir George,' she said condescendingly. 'We do not see you for months on end and then you disturb our country's business with trifles. How are your falcons, Royal Falconer?'

Sir George, visibly annoyed, answered, 'Even though Falconia Castle has no falcons anymore, my other work keeps me busy.'

'Oh, yes,' the queen replied, with the same condescending tone, 'I keep forgetting, you are supposed to be the head of my intelligence. Well, tell me! Is there any intelligence in Falconia?'

The queen tittered at her own joke, with all in the Throne Room except Sir George Potts joining in. Sir George waited with ill-disguised impatience for the noise to stop. 'We have just received a messenger pigeon from the mines.'

Queen Katerina suddenly looked serious. The mines were the wealth of Falconia and all reports from there were sent by horseback, which took two days, except for emergencies when pigeons were used, 'Well, what did it say?'

'A delegation of dwarfs wishes to speak to you at the main mine camp.'

'Dwarfs?' the queen exclaimed. 'There have been no dwarfs in Falconia for over two hundred years.'

'Two hundred and thirty-seven years ago they were decimated at the Battle of the Northern Gap and we have not seen or heard of them since,' Sir George stated.

'That says little for your intelligence,' the queen sneered. 'Well, what do they want?'

'They demand to speak to you.'

'Demand? Demand? No one demands of me! I will speak to them because I wish to find out what they want! NOT because they demanded of me,' the queen shouted. 'Send for them to come to me, now!'

'They will come no further than the mines, Your Majesty.'

The queen paused in thought, and then waved everyone away. 'Very well. We must prepare. Everyone leave me and send for Princess Scarlett and Captain Miland.' She turned to Sir George Potts. 'Thank you for this information. For once your intelligence is useful. Now you may go and eat the pigeon.'

The Royal Falconer suppressed a scowl, and bowed. 'Thank you, Your Majesty,' and turned and left with all the others.

The queen paced along the front of the dais as she waited for Princess Scarlett and Captain Miland. Princess Scarlett entered from one of the doors behind the throne and went to sit on her smaller throne on the dais. The captain entered through the main doors, walked up to the dais and bowed. The queen addressed the captain, leaving her back to her daughter as she did so. She told them what the Royal Falconer had said. She then ordered the captain. 'Bring six of your most trusted men and meet us at my reading room immediately.' The captain bowed. 'At once, Your Majesty,' then turned and left.

'Mother what are you planning to do?' Princess Scarlett enquired.

The queen smiled at her daughter, 'I am going to make those dwarfs wish that they had died out. What was it?' She paused. 'Two hundred and thirty-seven years ago.'

The queen's reading room was near her personal quarters and it was used by her, and before that by her predecessors, to study important documents before signing. It was not a large room and had narrow, square, wooden panels on three of the walls, and the fourth contained large glass windows to let in as much light as possible for reading. There was a table and just the one comfortable chair in there. When the queen and Princess Scarlett got there the captain and half a dozen guards were already there waiting. The queen opened the door with a click of her fingers and everyone crowded inside. The queen turned to the guards. 'If any one of you ever mentions what you will see and do today, all of you' — she emphasised the last words — 'I repeat, all of you, will be giving swimming lessons in the moat. Do you understand?' The guards all nodded and said, 'Yes, Your Majesty.'

Queen Katerina knocked twice on one of the wooden panels at the back of the room and part of the wall silently slid aside. It revealed a stairway leading down into what seemed to be an awfully dark, gaping hole. 'Follow me,' the queen said, and beckoned. She put out her left hand palm up. A bright flame suddenly appeared on her hand, lighting the way. They descended the stairs.

The long passage terminated in a cave on the side of a hill behind the castle and the town. Outside the cave was a small clearing surrounded by dense wood. It was still only early afternoon and the sun shone brightly in the clearing. The queen waved her hands twice in front of her face and a shimmering haze about ten feet in diameter appeared in front of them causing some mutterings among the guards. 'Silence! You will all follow me through the space mover. It will take us to the mines.' She then strode into the shimmering haze followed by the captain and her daughter and more nervously by the six guards.

They exited through a matching haze in a small valley in the mountains, all feeling exhausted. 'We will rest here for a little while,' the queen stated, as she waved her hands again making the haze disappear. 'A fast way to travel but extremely tiring.' She sat on a convenient rock. Her daughter joined her. 'What was that thing?' she asked.

'For want of a better name, I call it a space mover. It can move people and objects between two far places almost instantaneously, so our two-day trip only took seconds.'

Princess Scarlett frowned. 'I've been to Minesville before. It only took a day to get there.'

The queen sighed. 'It is the trip from Minesville into the mountains to the actual mines which is troublesome. The roads are not good.'

'Are you able to use these space movers anywhere?' the princess asked.

'No, I know of only two; this one and the one to the north

of Passville, which leads to outside of your grandparents' castle in Mayflor. When this problem and the problem you are working on are finished, I will show it to you.'

'Thank you, mother.'

The queen stood and clapped her hands. 'Up! We've still a mile to walk to get to the main mine camp.' She pointed to the west. 'That way.' She started walking down the valley which led in the direction she had pointed. The others got up and followed.

The queen was still looking resplendent when they entered the main mining camp situated in the valley area of the base of three adjoining mountains half an hour later. The rest of her party including her daughter were looking rather bedraggled. The mining camp consisted of about two dozen buildings of various sizes and there were several mine entrances in the mountainside. Miners were running from everywhere bowing and scraping to the queen. From inside the largest building in the camp a huge man six-feet, ten-inches tall, broad as an ox and in full armour emerged with a dozen partially armoured soldiers behind him. He bowed the best he could in his armour and then raised his visor. 'Your Majesty, we did not expect you so soon.'

The queen looked into the man's badly scarred face and smiled. 'Colonel Blayton, what is happening?'

'Nine dwarfs, Your Majesty. They say they have come to negotiate the return of the mines to their ownership.'

'They jest surely. They want me to give them the wealth of Falconia?'

'That's what they said. We are fortunate to have extra troops here as the monthly ore and gem shipment hasn't left for Minesville yet.'

'I doubt we will need them. Where are these dwarfs?'

The colonel pointed at the large building. 'In the main hall there. They are waiting for you.'

'What!' the queen shouted, 'Me go to them. Get them out here. Now!'

The colonel turned and ordered one of his men to go and fetch the dwarfs. Princess Scarlett, in the meantime, had tidied herself up and went to stand next to her mother. Captain Miland paraded his men behind them. The nine dwarfs came out of the main hall. The tallest was about four feet tall and the shortest about three feet. They all wore multicoloured clothing and had long, brown hair and beards. Each had a short sword at their side. The colonel's soldiers stood on either side of the dwarfs as they approached the queen. When they were six yards away from the queen, Colonel Blayton shouted, 'Stop! That's close enough.'

They halted and, as one, all bowed. The shortest one

there then took an extra step forward and spoke. 'Your Majesty, it is an honour to meet you. We did not expect you for at least two days.'

The queen looked down haughtily at him but did not speak. She gave a twirled wave of her hand to indicate he should continue and then crossed her arms. 'My name is Borin Steelhammer. My comrades and I represent the Northern Ranges Tribes of Dwarfs. We have lived literally in these mountains for over two thousand years and we have come to speak to you to tell you that we want these mines back.' The queen remained silent, so he continued, 'We understand Falconian prosperity depends on these mines, so please be assured that we will share the wealth of the mines with you, but you must understand, to us these are not just mines, but our heritage.'

The queen still didn't speak but just stood there looking at the dwarfs. Borin Steelhammer turned to exchange worried glances with his comrades who had started murmuring to each other. He turned back to the queen who uncrossed her arms and pointed behind Borin Steelhammer at the rest of the dwarfs. Lightning flew from her fingertips and an explosion blew half of the dwarfs into pieces killing them instantly. The colonel's men all dived for cover. She then scooped with her left hand and two of the surviving dwarfs flew twenty feet into the air and came down with a loud crunch and ceased moving. Borin Steelhammer, while this was happening, had drawn his sword and was charging at the queen while his other two comrades were standing stunned in place. The queen stared at Borin as he neared her. She closed her hands together slowly and he came to a halt, his face starting to turn red. Finally, the queen's hands fully closed and Borin Steelhammer's head imploded into a bloody mess. The queen turned to her daughter. 'Would you like to do one?'

'Oh, yes, please.' Princess Scarlett smiled, as she pointed at one of the two surviving dwarfs. He started to choke. His hands went to his throat as he struggled to breathe and he staggered staring with bulging eyes towards the princess. He slowly fell to his knees and he started to turn blue. About thirty seconds later he was dead still staring at the princess, who giggled. 'That was fun.' She laughed.

'Nicely done, very neat.' The queen smiled at her daughter and then turned to the visibly quaking last dwarf. She pointed at his feet and a small explosion blew him to the ground. He looked up at the queen from lying on his back and the queen smiled as she pointed again. Another small explosion occurred next to his head causing cuts to his face. He scrambled up as fast as he could as the queen aimed again at his feet. He jumped back and turned and started to run as fast as his small legs could move him. The queen aimed two more small explosions behind him for encouragement.

Princess Scarlett looked at her mother, surprised. 'You let him go?'

The queen smiled. 'Someone has to let the other dwarfs know our answer,' she replied.

While all this was happening, the soldiers, guards and miners watched in silence. The queen turned to address them. 'If any of you see any more of these vermin around the mines you are to kill them at once or inform the guards so that they can do so. I will be sending several wraiths to assist in spotting them both in the mountains and in the mines.' She turned to Colonel Blayton. 'Colonel, arrange for extra troops and patrols around the mines on a permanent basis and build some fortifications. We may have to give them a second lesson.'

The Colonel bowed. 'Yes, Your Majesty.'

The queen then looked around. 'Where's my mine manager?'

The mine manager, a short, stocky man with a shaved head, moved out from the crowd of miners. The queen continued, 'I am exceedingly disappointed in you allowing such a mess at my mines.' She indicated the dead dwarfs. 'Get it cleaned up immediately.'

The mine manager bowed. 'Yes, Your Majesty, immediately, Your Majesty.' He called several miners to help him.

'Well, we must be getting back to Falconia Castle.' The queen looked at her daughter, 'You still have that other problem that you must prepare for. Captain Miland, bring your men.' She led her group away from the mines back towards the valley with the space mover without another word.

The mine manager walked up to Colonel Blayton who was watching the queen's party leave. He said, 'Where the hell did she come from?'

Colonel Blayton answered with a wry smile, 'Yes, you're probably right.'

CHAPTER 9

Sir Philip and Jenny kept going after leaving the river for as long as possible before it grew dark. There was a reasonable path which led in a north-easterly direction from the bridge and they managed to put some distance between themselves and the bridge. They camped on the path itself without a fire. Sir Philip ate some cold lamb and Jenny had to make do with leaves from low branches. They still had several full water bags and Sir Philip poured some into his empty stew pot for Jenny to drink before drinking from a waterbag himself.

The next day they were up with the dawn. After a cold breakfast they headed off again. As the day wore on the path became less and less navigable although still heading in the right direction. Sir Philip noticed that Jenny had begun to get less skittish, but Sir Philip kept thinking he saw something insubstantial out of the corner of his eye, but whenever he looked directly at it there was nothing there. That afternoon they came across another stream and Sir Philip decided to set camp early as there was grass next to the stream for Jenny and signs of rabbits. He set a couple of snares and that night feasted on rabbit stew.

The next morning, he mounted Jenny and stroked her mane. 'Well, girl, by my calculations we should be in Harbourtown by sometime tomorrow afternoon and I promise that you'll get the best grain in town.' Jenny whinnied in approval. 'And I'll get to see Charlotte.' He was surprised at the warm feeling that thought gave him.

Late that afternoon he was riding through a particularly dense part of the forest, contemplating where he would camp for the night when, unexpectedly, two large scruffy men dressed in green stepped out from the forest onto the path before him. They were both armed. One was tall and slender with thinning black hair and carried an old sword. The other was an older man, tall, plump and muscular. He had red hair and carried a massive axe. He looked up at Sir Philip, smiled and spoke. 'Welcome, stranger! It is a beautiful day, is it not?'

Sir Philip immediately wary, looked down and replied,

'Well, it has been, until now at least. Please move aside so I may pass.'

The redheaded man smiled. 'Certainly, once you have paid the toll of' — he rubbed his chin — 'you look wealthy, five gold pieces.'

Sir Philip smiled also, while drawing his sword from its scabbard. 'Do you think you two are capable of taking it from me?'

The redheaded man's smile broadened. 'Much as I would like to say yes, the answer is no.' He raised his hand and pointed behind Sir Philip. 'But the two men behind you with arrows aimed at your back might be.' Sir Philip turned in his saddle. Two smaller men also dressed in green had entered the path behind him, both with notched bows and with their arrows pointed at him.

Sir Philip turned back to whom he assumed was the leader and stated, 'You do realise I am on a mission for the Queen of Falconia to the burgers of the free port of Harbourtown.'

The bandit smirked. 'In that case you should be good for ten gold pieces. I never did like the queen.'

Sir Philip gave a small laugh. 'I can understand that.' He knew he could beat the two men standing in front of him, but not the two bowmen behind him. Even his new, lighter, stronger armour wouldn't stop an arrow at that range. It looked as if he may have to pay the toll. He wondered if he had enough coins left.

Suddenly, one of the bowmen screamed. Sir Philip turned in his saddle. A wispy creature looking like a wavy column of smoke with eyes and a pair of claws was floating behind him clutching the bowman's blood-dripping heart in one of its claws. A gaping hole was in the bowman's chest and as his scream died, so did he and he slowly crumpled to the ground. The other bowman fired his arrow at the wraith which passed right through where its body should have been. The wraith reached out its other claw which entered the other bowman's chest and he too screamed as his heart was torn from his body and he collapsed to the ground. The first two bandits seeing what was happening forgot all about Sir Philip and fled for their lives. Sir Philip, fortunately (for him), had been trained in the methods of fighting various monsters and knew that to kill a wraith he had to stab it between its eyes. He dismounted from Jenny, his sword still in his hand. The wraith floated in front of him with a heart in each claw. It hissed, 'Stop, I've no wish to harm you. In fact, I just saved your life.'

'Why?'

'I cannot tell you.'

'Have you been following me?' The wraith didn't answer.

'Answer, or I'll thrust this sword between your eyes! Did the queen send you?' Sir Philip shouted.

The wraith showed no reaction. 'Is that how you will repay me for saving you?'

Sir Philip paused for a few seconds and nodded to himself. 'No, be gone then and stop following me, or even though you helped me, I will kill you.'

'I will leave you for now. We may or may not ever meet again,' and with that parting remark the wraith floated back into the forest.

Sir Philip made no attempt to follow the wraith as it had completely disappeared. He went and stroked Jenny's mane. 'And we thought we'd shaken the queen's shadows. It seems that she has more than human allies.'

He remounted Jenny and rode on a little way not wanting to camp next to the gruesome bodies of the bowmen, which he left for the night creatures to feast on. He finally found a camping spot a couple of miles further on, but he did not get any sleep that night.

Chapter 10

He searched the immediate area before he started off the next morning. There was no sign of robbers or wraiths. Jenny was back to being completely normal and she had no sign of the skittishness that had affected her before. He spotted the walls of Harbourtown late that afternoon. He knew when he was getting closer first by the number of seagulls about and then by the smell of the ocean. Harbourtown was situated at the end of the Northern Ranges. It was one of only two ports on the east coast of that part of the continent of Strasia, the other port being Thrackstown. The rest of the coastline consisted of steep cliffs and dangerous rocks, or had reefs that were not navigable. Between the ports and several miles inland was a huge area of arable land which was the main food crop source for all the major towns and kingdoms on the continent of Strasia. This area was called The Field and in its centre was the large lake called Lake Thracks. Canals from the lake had been built to help irrigate The Field.

Harbourtown was surrounded by a ten-foot wall without a glacis or moat as it had not fought with anyone ever. Some people wanted to knock the wall down, but the burgers who ruled Harbourtown were happy to have a proper boundary, especially at those times an illegal animal appeared. Sir Philip rode in the main gate and headed straight for the merchant quarter near the harbour, for that was where he knew he would find Charlotte. Charlotte owned an apothecary and herbal tea shop which had a large clientele. The shop stood out from the rest in the street because of the beautiful, white climbing rose which grew on the front wall. Sir Philip had been told when he was in Harbourtown the first time, that it had been planted by Charlotte's parents on her first birthday. When he entered her shop, she was wearing an apron over a pleasant floral dress, preparing an herbal infusion of chamomile tea for two older ladies who were sitting near the main window of the shop. As soon as she saw Sir Philip, she gave a little squeal of pleasure and called to one of her assistants to finish while she rushed over to give Sir Philip a big hug and kiss. Sir Philip returned the hug and kisses and said, smiling, 'I must stop wearing this armour, and the last time I gave you a kiss I was thrown in a dungeon.'

Charlotte looked at him in wide-eyed surprise. 'What?'

Philip looked around. In the shop were Charlotte's two assistants and five customers drinking tea and eating some of Charlotte's herbal scones. 'I need to talk to you in private,' he whispered.

Charlotte, who was a perfect twin of her sister, Princess Scarlett, except for their personalities, led him through the kitchen and up the stairs to her private quarters. She had told her assistants to look after the shop until it closed, which would be soon. One of her assistants, Pat, a plump, older lady with hair that was beginning to grey, had looked after Charlotte after her parents had been murdered. She lived in rooms behind the kitchen while the other, a young girl called Jayne about Charlotte's age, lived with her parents. They were both extremely trustworthy and Charlotte knew she could rely on them completely.

Charlotte and Sir Philip sat at a small table in Charlotte's parlour. She asked, 'What's all this about? What do you mean you were arrested for kissing me?'

'I met your sister' Philip replied.

'What sister?' Charlotte asked, astonished.

'Sit down and listen.' Philip related all the events of the last week. Charlotte gasped when she heard that he had been thrown in the dungeon, was surprised to learn that the pendant she had given Sir Philip had minor powers and was positively horrified when she heard about the robbers and the wraith, especially when she heard that a wraith was one of the creatures that could easily penetrate Sir Philip's armour. 'This armour will stop most sword blows except maybe a really powerful thrust. Won't stop a strong axe blow, of course, and a well-aimed arrow could penetrate it.' They were both silent for several minutes when Sir Philip had finished.

Charlotte broke the silence. 'So, I am the daughter of the King and Queen of Falconia. A princess.'

Sir Philip nodded, 'It certainly seems like it. What are your earliest memories?'

'I just have the usual childhood memories. My parents, Stephen and Julie, were murdered and robbed while travelling between here and Thrackstown when I was eight and Pat, a close friend of my parents looked after me until I took over the shop. Burger Rowles, my godfather, and Burger Thompson also helped raise me. I remember a strange creature called Dobbin from my infancy. He has the head of a horse, the torso of a man and the legs of a goat. He still helps me find herbs when I go deeper into the forest and acts as my bodyguard while I am there. He's not allowed near Harbourtown and would be executed if he came here. I've always, as far as I can remember, had this necklace with this half medallion.' She fingered her medallion, which was a half-circle with a jagged edge looking as if it had been torn from the other half. It had a strange symbol on it that looked like a part of a star and moon. 'And I was given this silver bracelet with the heads of two dolphins at the ends, by my parents just before they were murdered.' She touched the bracelet on her arm. 'My mother, Julie, had some minor powers which she never dared let anyone but my father and me know about, and a large knowledge of herb lore which she passed on to me. My father was a successful silversmith. When they were murdered by bandits, they left me quite well off and I have expanded my mother's shop while keeping a small percentage of my father's business, although letting it be taken over by his journeymen and apprentices.'

'An interesting story,' Sir Philip said, thoughtfully rubbing his chin. 'I think it would be a good idea to talk to your friend, Dobbin, in the morning. He might know something useful.'

'He lives in a cave in the forest. We'll go and see him

tomorrow,' Charlotte replied. 'You can spend the night in the spare room. It's next door to Pat's.'

'No,' Sir Philip shook his head, 'I have to stable and look after Jenny and it will be very late by the time I have finished. I will stay at the inn next to the stable and see you first thing tomorrow. Bye until then.' He gave her a kiss on the cheek and left.

CHAPTER 11

The next morning in half armour of breast and back plate and helmet, he rode to the apothecary. The sun was out, and it looked like it was going to be a pleasantly warm day. Charlotte, wearing her riding clothes of blouse, jacket, jodhpurs and boots, was waiting for him with her small piebald horse called Maria. Charlotte mounted Maria and Sir Philip took his helmet off and gave her a kiss on the cheek. They both rode out of the south gate towards the forest. They rode several miles into the heavily treed forest until they came to a clearing with a cave set in a small hill. The clearing contained several logs that could be used as seats and there was an empty fire pit in the centre. Several large tools were outside the cave entrance. They dismounted leaving their horses untethered. Charlotte called out, 'Dobbin, it's me and I've bought a friend. We need to speak to you.'

Dobbin came out of the cave. It was eight foot tall and tremendously imposing. Sir Philip, whose training had taught him about strange creatures, stood amazed. He had never seen or heard of anything like what he was seeing now. Dobbin's head was that of a large brown horse. This was situated above a massive human torso with extremely muscular arms. Its legs were the largest and strongest looking goat's legs Sir Philip had ever seen. It was wearing what looked like a skirt made from a sack which covered it from its stomach to its thighs. As it entered the clearing from the cave, it moved its head round inspecting the forest. 'Greetings, Mistress Charlotte, Greetings, Mistress Charlotte's friend.' Its voice was very hoarse and came out as a whisper. 'This visit is a surprise; I did not expect to see you until next week. How can I help you?'

Charlotte answered, 'Greetings, Dobbin. I hope you are well.' Dobbin nodded. 'We need you to tell us exactly what happened when I arrived here from Falconia.'

Dobbin was stunned. It sat down on a log. 'How do you know this?' It gesticulated with surprise. 'It is supposed to be a secret that can never be revealed.'

Sir Philip and Charlotte also sat on logs; Charlotte took

Dobbin's hand. 'My friend, Sir Philip, has just returned from Falconia. He met with Queen Katerina who told him that I was kidnapped by a gang of ruffians as a baby. Also, that I am a princess there and Queen Katerina and my sister would like to have me back in their loving arms.'

Dobbin laughed, at least Charlotte and Sir Philip thought it was a laugh. It sounded more like a loud bray. 'The queen would like no better news than that you are dead. I was ordered by her to take you far away and make sure you never returned. She told me I was not allowed to kill you, but if someone else tried, I was not to defend you. I was not even given food or milk for you. Fortunately, your midwife gave me some without the queen's knowledge before I left. I was in this very part of the forest when I came across your mother. I had been injured in a fall and was limping badly. Your mother fixed my hoof' — Dobbin pointed at its left goatlike hoof — 'and asked me who you were. I felt bad about lying to her, but I told her you were just a baby I had found in the woods. She told me that she was barren and asked if she could take you. I said "yes" thinking that you would never find out who you really were and that I was helping the two of you; but now you know, I do not know what to do.'

'Why did you stay here in the forest?' Charlotte asked.

Dobbin sat silent for a few seconds, then continued in

a louder voice, 'I was one of several experiments of the queen. When I left, there were five of us, all of us living in a locked, underground cellar, never seeing the light of day except for the ones of us that lived in the moat.'

Sir Philip interrupted, 'The moat monsters? There are two now.'

Dobbin gave its head a shake, its mane flowing in the breeze. 'Who knows how many have died or how many new creatures that evil witch has created. I do know that I didn't want to go back and live in that cellar again, so I found this cave and I stayed. Your mother was incredibly kind to me and brought you to visit and as long as I do not wander close to Harbourtown, I have been happy here.'

'A very interesting and pleasant story.' The red-headed bandit who had tried to rob Sir Philip on his journey to Harbourtown came out of the trees. He waved a hand at Sir Philip, 'You seem to make a habit of hanging around with monsters.' He looked around. 'Your smoky friend's not with you, though.'

Sir Philip stood and answered with a sneer, 'Haven't you learnt your lesson? Go away and you may live.'

The bandit spread his hands and grinned. 'No, I was thinking that we would dispose of you and the monster and then tie up the pretty girl and take her back to her mother.' At these words a half dozen men, including the tall, balding man from Sir Philip's previous encounter in the forest, came out of the forest behind the red-headed man. They were all armed with swords, axes or clubs and, like their leader, all dressed in green.

Charlotte stood and drew herself to her full height. 'I am a Princess of Falconia. You will not harm my companions or me.' Charlotte attempted to make her voice extremely authoritarian.

The red-headed man gave a loud guffaw which was echoed by his men. 'Sure, that's really impressive.' He shook his head and continued, 'There should be a large reward for you. Your friend here will die.' He gestured towards Sir Philip. 'He has already cost me my two bowmen and who will miss a monster? And who would have thought that we would ever be helping the Queen of Falconia?' He laughed and turned to make sure his men were laughing also. They were.

While Charlotte and the robber were talking, Sir Philip was slowly inching towards Jenny, who also was moving slowly towards him. When Jenny was only two yards away, he made a final dash and pulled the battle axe from its holder on the saddle. He threw it to Dobbin. 'Dobbin, catch.' Dobbin caught the axe and began to swivel it expertly around above his head. 'Thank you, I haven't used one of these in years.' Sir Philip then pulled his sword from its scabbard on his saddle — he did not have time to grab his helmet or shield — and he and Dobbin both began to advance on the robbers.

The red-haired man's men halted. From advancing on three unarmed people, they now faced a large knight with a sword and an even larger creature with a battle axe. Dobbin, having the larger reach, got close to one of the robbers first. He was red headed like their leader and was armed with a sword. Dobbin one-handedly raised the axe above his head and brought it down towards the robber's head. The robber raised his sword to block the stroke and his sword was snapped in two by the axe, which then continued its downward stroke to split his head in half. His hair did little to disguise the colour of the blood that poured from his head. Sir Philip, in the meantime, moved close to a man armed only with a club. Unfortunately for the robber, a club is not much good against a sword. Sir Philip slashed his sword across the man's stomach, slicing him open. The man dropped his club, as he was much more interested in stopping his intestines from falling out than fighting. Sir Philip let his slash continue hitting another robber on the upper right arm near the elbow. His arm was almost cut in two. The robber dropped the axe he was holding and started running, his arm flapping unnaturally as he ran.

Dobbin's next swing almost decapitated his opponent, the tall, balding man from the forest, who fell with blood gushing from his neck. Disastrously for Dobbin, his follow-through left his back turned to the robber leader. The robbers' leader with both hands on his axe slashed at Dobbin with all his strength and his axe imbedded itself in the centre of Dobbin's back and stuck. Dobbin went down with blood spouting from the wound.

The robbers' leader then picked up the sword of Dobbin's last victim. Sir Philip was now outnumbered three to one — one armed with an axe, one a sword and one a club. 'Try to take him alive, I want his death to be slow and painful,' the robbers' leader snarled. They spread out to make it harder for Sir Philip to attack them. Charlotte suddenly screamed. Everyone stopped to look at her. She threw a packet towards the robber closest to her, a bald, small but thickset man armed with an axe. It burst in his face and he started to sneeze uncontrollably. He collapsed to the ground still sneezing. Sir Philip used the diversion to thrust his sword at the man armed with a club. The sword stabbed him in the throat and blood started surging from the wound. The robber tried to stop the bleeding with his hands as he slowly sank to the ground.

Sir Philip smiled as he advanced on the robbers' leader.

'Just you and me. I will try to take you alive as I want you to die slowly on the scaffold. Whatever happens, I promise to make it painful.'

The red-headed robbers' leader looked around trying to find a way to escape. There was none. He threw down his sword and knelt with his arms thrown wide. 'I yield. You are a knight; you cannot kill an unarmed man.'

Sir Philip stopped with his sword at the throat of the robbers' leader and spat at the man, 'Coward, I will take you back to be tried. I'd rather see you hang anyway.'

The last robber's sneezing had subsided, but he was still on the ground. Charlotte was kneeling next to Dobbin whose wound was still gushing blood. Sir Philip ordered the two surviving robbers to lie next to each other on their stomachs with their hands above their heads.

Sir Philip moved close to Charlotte and Dobbin. 'How's Dobbin?' he asked. Charlotte looked up, tears trickling heavily from her eyes and down her cheeks and shook her head.

Dobbin looked up at Charlotte. 'I am finished. I thank you and your mother for making my years here happy. DO NOT TRUST THE QUEEN! She wants you dead.' It looked at Sir Philip 'You fought well, Sir Knight.'

Sir Philip answered, 'Not as well as you. I owe you my life.'

Dobbin nodded and died in Charlotte's arms. Sir Philip turned on the robbers. 'You two can dig a grave. Come on, do it now,' Sir Philip snarled. There were digging tools near the entrance of Dobbin's cave and Sir Philip gave them a pick and a shovel while holding his sword and shield and watching them attentively. While the robbers were digging, Sir Philip whispered to Charlotte, 'Thanks for the sneezes. What was that stuff?'

'It was a mixture of peppers, thyme, cumin, chilli and tobacco. I carry various herbs and mixtures of herbs for various purposes.'

Sir Philip looked astonished. 'Wow, what was the purpose of that mix?'

'To put off unwanted suitors. You notice I haven't used it on you' — she paused — 'yet.' She smiled.

While they were talking the robbers were doing the same. Suddenly, the one who had been sneezing threw a shovel full of dirt in Sir Philip's face and attacked him with the shovel. Sir Philip backed away dropping his shield so he could wipe the dirt from his face and then countered the shovel with his sword. He knocked the robber to the ground and stood over him, cursing himself for his inattentiveness. While this was happening, the robbers' leader dropped the pick and ran towards the forest. He stopped at the edge and gave Charlotte and

Sir Philip a rude gesture. 'I will get both of you yet,' he shouted. 'Just you wait and see.' He then disappeared into the forest. Sir Philip decided not to follow as he would have had to leave Charlotte alone with the other robber.

They made the remaining robber finish digging the grave for Dobbin while hobbled with a rope. They buried Dobbin with what ceremony they could manage. They buried Sir Philip's battle axe with Dobbin. During the ceremony, they left the robber tied up. They then untied the hobbling rope on the prisoner while leaving his hands tied so he could walk while they rode back to Harbourtown. Sir Philip also tied a rope around the prisoner's neck, tying the other end to his saddle pommel. They left the dead robbers where they had fallen. On the way back, they came upon the robber who had his arm almost cut in two. He had bled to death.

CHAPTER 12

They rode back into Harbourtown through the south gate. The guards on duty challenged them because of their prisoner. Sir Philip explained that he was part of a renegade gang that prowled in the forest and they were going to turn him over to the constables. Charlotte knew where the constables' barracks was and led them into the centre of the town. People turned to watch them pass. It was not every day someone was led into Harbourtown tied and on a leash. When they arrived at the barracks, they turned their prisoner over to a black-clad constable sergeant and his associate. Charlotte then left to return to her apothecary, while Sir Philip stayed to help the constables question the prisoner.

They discovered his name was Tom and, when faced

with the well-stocked torture chamber and knowing that he had been abandoned by his leader instead of been helped as promised with his attack on Sir Philip, he told them almost everything they wanted to know. The leader of the gang was a man called "Charlie the Mean" and he was a mean, vicious, bad-tempered brute. The constables were very interested when they heard Charlotte was the daughter of the Queen of Falconia and started to question Sir Philip, who declined to answer questions about Charlotte, stating that the topic should be left until another time. They also learnt the location of Charlie's camp and now that he had lost eight men, he only had four left and that one of them was badly wounded.

The constables promised Sir Philip that the next morning they would organise an attack on the camp. They then told Sir Philip they would have to call a senior burger to arrange for charges to be laid against Tom. The senior burger that was summoned was the same one Sir Philip had met when he had fought the manticore, Burger Rowles. When Burger Rowles arrived, he was told the full story. He then went and talked to Tom privately and afterwards he ordered that Charlotte be summoned at once.

Charlotte arrived at the barracks. She had changed out of her riding clothes and now wore a respectable blue, knee-length dress. She curtsied to the burger who was sitting at a desk. 'I believe you have summoned me, Burger Rowles. What may I do for you?'

Burger Rowles looked at her stone-faced. 'Princess Charlotte.' Charlotte flinched at the title. It was the first time anyone had used it. 'It has been reported that you have been consorting with monsters. This is against the laws of Harbourtown. You may be imprisoned or banished.'

Charlotte physically staggered at the statement. 'What! Dobbin was not a monster. He was a peaceful creature,' Charlotte shouted.

Burger Rowles slammed his fist on the desk. 'Was he human? No. Therefore he, I mean "it", was a monster. Moreover, it has been reported that it killed two humans.'

Charlotte screamed, 'They were trying to kill us.'

Burger Rowles half rose from his seat. 'The prisoner said all they were planning to do was to return you to your mother and that the monster attacked them first.' He turned to Sir Philip. 'And I believe you are not entirely innocent in this.'

Sir Philip was so shocked that he sat down, shaking his head. 'So, you are saying these men were innocent!'

Burger Rowles replied, sitting back down, 'No, of course not.' His manner softened. 'This band of cutthroats has been terrorising the area for years. In fact, it is believed that it was this gang that murdered your parents. They were close friends of mine.' He made this last comment to Charlotte. 'I'm just emphasising that you two could be charged also.' He sighed. 'You won't be. We haven't forgotten how you helped the town by killing the manticore and Charlotte is a great asset to the sick and poorer people of the town. However, you may consider this an official warning.' He raised his voice, 'Dobbin was an illegal monster that would have been executed if it had come to Harbourtown and I'm telling you very plainly, be more careful with what you consort with in future.' He turned to Sir Philip. 'Will you be accompanying the constables on the raid on the bandit camp in the morning?'

'Yes.' Sir Philip nodded, still shocked by his official warning. 'Most definitely. I wish to see this Charles brought to justice and hung.'

Meantime, back in Falconia, the wraith was reporting to Princess Scarlett in the queen's laboratory. The laboratory was exceptionally large and had been painted an off-white colour. The floor consisted of grey slate. It was one of the biggest rooms in the castle. There were numerous shelves containing lots of different sized jars, almost all containing chemicals or strange and magical items. Cauldrons of all sizes were either on the floor or on one of four large benches. There were also several chairs and stools. From the room were several doors including a large iron one which was locked. The wraith informed Princess Scarlett of the ambush in the forest and how it had helped Sir Philip. Also, how it had been ordered to leave, but it was obvious that Sir Philip was heading to the Free Port of Harbourtown.

The princess dismissed the wraith, then sat for a while thinking. She went to one of her mother's larger cauldrons which she set upon a burning hearth. She mixed several liquids from large jars around the laboratory into the cauldron and when the mixture was boiling, she finally sprinkled a strange powder into the cauldron while muttering some unintelligible words. She finished with the words, 'Harpies appear!'

Two grotesque creatures appeared before her. Both were about six feet tall and looked like ravens except for their heads which both looked like bald, ugly hags. They were both jet black and had huge claws and sharp teeth. They both had large powerful eyes and they both drooled. They cackled in unison, 'Yes, mistress, what would you have us do?'

Princess Scarlett smiled. 'I want you to kill someone. Preferably extremely painfully. Do you know how to get to Harbourtown?' They both nodded. 'There is a girl there that looks just like me. She is to die.'

One of the harpies croaked, 'We can find Harbourtown without a problem, mistress. We will kill her as painfully as we can. We will enjoy that, but if she looks just like you how will we know we are not killing you by mistake?'

The princess thought for a few seconds. 'I will remain in Falconia until you report she is dead, and we will have a password. "Belladonna" is a nice, poisonous word.'

The other harpy cackled, 'She is as good as dead, mistress. We fly at once.' They both flew out of an open high window in one of the walls. Princess Scarlett smiled an evil smile and went to bed to dream happy dreams of her sister being torn to pieces.

CHAPTER 13

The next day Burger Rowles led a dozen armoured constables and Sir Philip in full armour into the forest. They had Tom with them tied to a horse. He had been promised a lesser sentence if he led them to the robbers' camp. They rode for more than two hours into the forest until they came close to the clearing where the camp was. Two of the constables dismounted and scouted the camp carefully on foot. They soon returned. One reported to the burger, 'The camp seems deserted, sir.'

Burger Rowles, Sir Philip and the constables rode into the obviously deserted camp. The burger ordered Sir Philip and his men, except for two constables who were left guarding Tom, to search the camp. There were four small, wooden huts in the camp and a central lean-to, which had obviously been used as a kitchen area. One of the constables found a wounded robber in one of the huts. His throat had been cut. Burger Rowles shook his head and commented, 'I suppose that's one way to stop him from talking to us.' They also found what was left of their treasure pit. It was in one of the huts and was a hole four feet deep and three feet by three feet wide. They knew it was the treasure pit as it was not completely empty. There were still several inches of silver and gold coins, some gems and some jewellery at the bottom.

Burger Rowles and Sir Philip stood at the edge of the pit looking down at the remaining treasure. Burger Rowles shook his head and said, 'They certainly robbed a lot of people over the years to accumulate this much loot and this is just what they left.'

Sir Philip answered with a wry grin, 'I'm just glad they didn't waste any of it on better weapons.'

They both chuckled. The burger said to Sir Philip, 'There are only four of them left. They obviously couldn't carry all their loot.' He turned to Tom who had been bought into the camp. 'Do you know where they are likely to go?' Tom shook his head. The burger continued, 'Sir Philip, would you please take three of my men and return to Harbourtown with this piece of filth.' He looked at Tom who fell to his knees.

'You'll still be merciful with me, please. I did show you the way to the camp,' Tom pleaded.

'Yes, we keep our bargains.' He turned back to Sir Philip. 'Also take back the rest of the robbers' hoard; well, we can't leave it here while I take the rest of the men after them. They have almost a day's start on us and it looks like they have several horses, but they will be loaded down by the treasure they are carrying, and we may yet catch them.'

Sir Philip replied, 'Certainly, sir.'

Burger Rowles ordered his nine remaining constables to mount up to go after Charlie and his cronies. Sir Philip left one of his constables guarding Tom, while he and the other two loaded the rest of the treasure into sacks, which they tied to the saddle pommels on the constable's horses. When they had finished, they retied Tom's hands behind him and retied him to his horse. A rope was also tied to his horse's bridle which was attached to Jenny's saddle pommel to make sure he could not try to escape, and they set off on their journey back to Harbourtown.

⁂

Meanwhile in Harbourtown, Charlotte was shopping for exotic herbs from overseas for the apothecary in the marketplace next to the harbour. She was wearing the same floral dress that she wore when Sir Philip returned to Harbourtown and she carried a cane basket. Unlike the market in Falconia, this market was full of people and merchants and was full of the noise of people bargaining and the smells of strange food cooking. Charlotte headed straight for the specific stalls where she usually bought some of the more unusual and exotic herbs that she used in her medicines and teas. There was a strong smell of the sea and many of the stalls sold fish. There was also beef from Concordia and stalls selling everything from pots and pans to carpets, expensive jewellery and clothes. However, this day she was in a slight daze, still being dreadfully upset about Dobbin and angry about the way Burger Rowles had spoken about him. Even so, she was having a friendly haggle with one of the merchants who sold herbs from the eastern islands.

Up above the market hidden in a low cloud the two harpies were hovering. Their large eyes were extraordinarily sharp and it did not take them long to spot Charlotte. One hag croaked to the other, 'There she is. Shall we go straight down and grab her?'

'Why not' the other answered. 'I have just seen a

school of three or four sharks about a mile out to sea. It will be fun watching them tear her to pieces.' They both laughed at the thought.

They both dived down towards Charlotte in the market. They screeched a high-pitched cry as they dived. The crowds of people in the market looked up, screamed and, panicking, ran in all directions for cover. Even the market's two patrolling constables ran. Charlotte dropped her basket and started to run back towards her apothecary. The two harpies, ignoring everyone else flew towards her. One grabbed her by her shoulders in its large claws and lifted her into the air tearing her dress as it did so. The harpies then flew upwards. When the harpy carrying Charlotte was about three hundred feet in the air she let go. Charlotte started to fall. She screamed as she fell. When she had dropped about a hundred feet the harpies caught her. Each grabbing one of her arms and once more they flew up towards the sky. 'That was fun,' one croaked. 'We should do that again.'

The other gave a cackled laugh and answered, 'Why not.' They let go again and once more Charlotte fell towards the ground, screaming. This time they did not catch her until there was only ten feet before she hit the now deserted market's paving. Charlotte had thought she was going to die. The harpies then started to fly towards and then over the sea.

Charlotte managed to swallow; tears were pouring down her face. She asked in a low, shaky voice, 'Why? Why are you doing this?'

The harpies cackled, 'For some reason, Scarlett, the Princess of Falconia, doesn't like you. Probably because you look like her,' one answered.

'She won't look like anything pretty soon,' the other said. They both cackled with laughter.

They continued flying out to sea with the harpies continuing to taunt her. 'There they are,' one laughed. She used her spare claw to point at the sharks. 'We'd better go down a lot closer. We wouldn't want her to get hurt when we drop her amongst the sharks.'

Charlotte gasped, 'Sharks?'

'Yes, we will watch them tear you to pieces and then eat you. It should be fun.'

The first harpy cackled to the other, 'We had better make her bleed a bit so the sharks will be sure to attack her.'

'Yes,' the other replied. 'Let's tear out a bit of her hair for a souvenir and a few bloody scratches won't hurt us at least.' They both gave their cackling laugh as they tore out a lock of Charlotte's hair and scratched her arms, so blood flowed down them.

They then dived down to two yards above the water and dropped Charlotte amid the three sharks. Charlotte screamed for help as she began to tread water. One of the sharks swam under her ready to rise and sink its teeth into her. Suddenly the shark was flying through the air. Charlotte watched as it was raised about six feet before crashing back down back into the water. The two other sharks swam at Charlotte and then crashed into each other as a giant, jet-black dolphin rammed one shark into the other. A second, also jet-black, giant dolphin attacked the shark that had been flying. The shark swam away quickly as did the two that had been rammed. They knew when they were outclassed.

The harpies watched in horror; their plan had been thwarted. One of them dived towards Charlotte in order to grab her. Just before it did, one of the dolphins leapt out of the water and grabbed the harpy's claw with its teeth. It dived back down with the harpy's claw and the harpy attached still in its teeth under the water. The other dolphin swam in front of Charlotte to guard her and watched the other harpy that was hovering above them. A couple of minutes later the other harpy floated to the surface very, very dead. It had been drowned. The live harpy screamed and pointed her claw at Charlotte and cried, 'We will get you yet. Your days are numbered.' It turned and flew off towards Falconia.

The sharks, smelling the body of the dead harpy, finally got their meal. One of the dolphins swam up under Charlotte so that she could grab hold of its dorsal fin and started the swim towards the shore. The other dolphin followed. When they were about fifty feet from the shore, the following dolphin chirruped at Charlotte and nudged her arm. It disappeared. The dolphin that was towing Charlotte then also chirruped at her and went to nudge her arm. Charlotte suddenly realised that they weren't nudging her arm but the silver bracelet with the dual dolphin heads. As soon as the second dolphin's nose touched the bracelet, it too disappeared. Charlotte swam the rest of the way towards the beach. On the beach were a burger and four constables as well as a small crowd of the townsfolk. Charlotte, bleeding and ragged, walked from the ocean and collapsed to her knees. She spoke to the burger, 'Thank you for coming to help me.'

The burger replied haughtily, 'We are not here to help you, but to arrest you for consorting with monsters.' He gestured to the constables. 'Take her to the cells.'

'What?' Charlotte gasped.

Ignoring her protests, two of the constables grabbed her by the arms and dragged her, protesting, off the beach.

CHAPTER 14

The hearing occurred later that afternoon in the courthouse next to the town hall. Charlotte, despite her young age, was still a prominent citizen of Harbourtown. Many of Harbourtown's population had been helped by her herbal remedies and, before that, those of her mother. For years her parents had been leading citizens. Her father had been a burger as well as a silversmith, so she therefore had her hearing very promptly (Harbourtown also boasted that any one arrested would have a trial within forty-eight hours although the court's decision could take a lot longer). She consequently had a lot of support in the court which was bulging at the seams with people after the news of the morning's events spread around the town. All the seats had been taken and people were standing everywhere and even outside, except for the front of the court where the actual trial took place. Black-clad constables stood between the crowd and the front of the court to keep control. The burger who had arrested her as well as two other burgers sat as judges — all serious charges were presided over by three burgers. The burger who had arrested her was Burger Jackson, an old, grizzled, grumpy, white-haired man (burgers were elected for life or until they wished to retire and there were fifteen burgers in Harbourtown). He got up to speak and pointed a bony finger at Charlotte as he addressed the assembly, 'We are here to judge Charlotte Silver who is charged with consorting with monsters. She was given an official warning only yesterday and yet today she was seen flying off with two harpies and swimming with two giant dolphins.' He turned to her, 'How do you plead?'

Charlotte, standing in the dock with her hands shackled in front of her, was so shocked all she could do was stand there with her mouth open. She was still wearing the same dress that she was wearing when she was dragged to the courthouse. She had lost her shoes. The scratches on her arms had stopped bleeding but were looking very red and angry. A patch of blood showed in her hair on the left side of her head where the lock of hair had been torn out. A large rotund, dark-haired man wearing the red and gold uniform of a burger stood up from the front row of the spectators. 'She pleads not guilty of course. This entire trial is a farce.'

Burger Jackson snarled and turned to him, 'Burger Thompson, what has this to do with you?'

'I am defending my client, if she'll have me.' He bowed towards Charlotte, who nodded, giving a sigh of relief. She needed someone on her side. Burger Thompson was an old friend of her father's. He pushed past the constables and went to stand by her side. 'We definitely refute these ridiculous charges.' He began to count off his fingers. 'Firstly, Charlotte was not consorting with harpies. In fact, they were trying to kill her, as witnessed by many of our fellow citizens here.' There was a murmur of agreement from the spectators. 'Secondly, if swimming or being friendly with dolphins is illegal, there are many people here in Harbourtown who should be charged too. Virtually all the sailors and fishermen, for starters, and myself as well.' There was another murmur of agreement in the court. 'Thirdly, and finally, this court does not have the power to try a Princess of Falconia.' There were shocked cries of surprise from all around the court. This was not general knowledge.

One of the shocked cries had come from Burger

Jackson. He stood and glared at Charlotte as he spoke to Burger Thompson. 'Then why has she been living here all this time under an assumed name?'

'That is no business of yours,' Burger Thompson declared, 'or anyone else here. You just need to drop the charges.'

Just then Sir Philip burst into the back of the court, shouting, 'What's going on here?' He pushed his way to the front of the spectators. 'Why has Charlotte Silver been arrested?' he shouted at the three burgers. This caused even more disorder in the courtroom.

Burger Thompson raised calming hands and shouted so he could be heard, 'Calm down, Sir Philip, Burger Jackson was just going to drop the charges.'

Burger Jackson stood banging his gavel. 'Silence! Silence!' The noise abated and he continued, 'No, I wasn't! There is no way I was going to do anything like that.' He paused and looked around the courtroom. 'However, I will suspend them until further investigations into this matter can be made.' He turned to face Charlotte. 'You have not been found innocent, Charlotte Silver or Princess Falconia or whatever you want to call yourself.' He uttered his next words slowly and deliberately, 'You ... will ... face ... justice.' He turned and left the court via a door near the front of the court, followed by the other two burgers.

One of the constables unlocked and removed the shackles on Charlotte's wrists and she ran to Sir Philip. She was going to put her arms around him but had the same problem as she always did when he was in full armour, although he had left his helmet behind in the constables' barracks. He had gone to the court immediately from the barracks next door when he had heard about the trial after arriving back in Harbourtown. Sir Philip kissed the top of her head and said, 'He doesn't seem to like you.'

Burger Thompson was standing next to them. 'He doesn't. His wife died from an attack by an amphisbaena' — Sir Philip looked puzzled — 'a two-headed poisonous snake. Charlotte's mother, Julie, tried to help her with herbal medicine but that,' he continued in a whisper only Sir Philip and Charlotte could hear, 'and even her extra powers couldn't help. Burger Jackson thinks she could have tried harder and blamed her partially for his wife's death. He also hates anything he thinks of as a monster and doesn't believe there could be friendly ones.'

Charlotte sighed. 'Let's go home, I've had an awful day and I hurt all over.' The three of them left the courtroom. Most of the spectators wished Charlotte the best and said that they knew that she would be found innocent. They all wanted to know when and how she had become

Princess Charlotte of Falconia. Burger Thompson addressed the crowd, stating that when it was all settled everything would be explained to the populace; and ordered several constables to make sure the three of them could leave without trouble. When the three of them reached Charlotte's apothecary, it was closed. Pat, still in the front of the shop, opened the door for them. Pat made them all a cup of lemon balm tea to relax them and tended to Charlotte's injuries. Charlotte told them what had happened to her with the harpies and dolphins that morning. Sir Philip and Burger Thompson both looked at the bracelet. The burger said, 'It looks like your mother's gift saved your life, but how is it you are a princess of Falconia?' Sir Philip told him what had happened in Falconia and what Dobbin had told them before he had died. He left out his journey and the encounter with the wraith.

'So, you were bought here by a monster,' Burger Thompson exclaimed.

'Dobbin was NOT A MONSTER!' Charlotte screamed. 'He was a happy, friendly, beautiful creature.'

'Okay, I'm sorry,' Burger Thompson stated, while lifting his hands in a placating manner. 'Don't forget I was one of the very few people whom your mother trusted enough to tell that she had strange powers.' He looked at her neck.

'I wonder if your medallion does anything,' he added, trying to change the subject.

Charlotte answered, 'Dobbin told me that I had this when he brought me here from Falconia.'

Sir Philip looked thoughtful. 'A mystery for another time.' He then told them all about the camp and what happened there. 'The big question, however, is how do we stop the queen and your sister from killing you?'

Charlotte answered excitedly, 'There is a hermit who lives in the mountains who is said to have great knowledge. We could go and ask his advice.'

Sir Philip nodded. 'It couldn't hurt.'

Burger Thompson smiled. 'Famous last words.'

Meanwhile, in the laboratory of the Queen of Falconia, Princess Scarlett looked up from an experiment and watched the harpy fly in through the window in the roof and then land in front of her. 'Good news, I trust. Where is your sister?'

The harpy looked down, not meeting Princess Scarlett's eyes. 'My sister is dead; the girl has strong magic and helpers on her side.'

'Has! Has!' Princess Scarlett screamed, turning vivid

red. 'You mean she's not dead?'

'No, mistress, she still lives. We were beaten,' the harpy cackled, looking at the floor.

'What!' Princess Scarlett screamed again and pointed her fingers at the harpy. Green lightning discharged from her fingers hitting the harpy in the chest. It was then the harpy's turn to scream as its skin started to bubble. The bubbles got bigger and burst, leaving green slime oozing from its body. Soon all that was left of her was a puddle of green slime on the floor. Princess Scarlett saw something floating on top of the slime. She bent down for a closer look. Floating on the slime was the lock of hair that had been torn from Charlotte's head. Princess Scarlett picked up the hair and held it against her own, it was a perfect match. 'Hmm, this would be my sister's,' she murmured thoughtfully. She went to a shelf and lifted down an empty jar. She put the hair in the lidded jar, patted it and put it back on the shelf. She then left, going to do some extra study in the queen's library.

CHAPTER 15

The next morning there was a knock at the door. Sir Philip, who had slept on the shop floor, rose to open it. A constable stood there. It was one of the men who had returned with him the previous day. Sir Philip said cheerfully, 'Hi, Jim, what news?'

Jim, a tall, thin, brown-haired man replied, ticking off statements on his fingers, 'Well, we threw Tom back into the cells. As we've promised not to hang him, he'll probably be sent to the Thracks Lake farms as a slave for the rest of his life. Burger Rowles isn't back yet. We've got the jewellery that we brought back from the robbers' camp on tables in the town hall, which is the actual reason for my visit. As we think that Charlotte's parents may have been murdered and robbed by this group of brutal thieves, she is to be one of the people we will be asking to go and see if she can recognise anything.'

Sir Philip replied, 'I will bring her myself when she has risen and eaten breakfast.'

Jim answered, 'Thank you. I will see you there.' He left.

Charlotte came down the stairs already dressed for the day in a green skirt and white blouse. 'Who was that?'

'One of the constables. They want you to go and view the property we brought back from the robbers' camp yesterday. In case any of it belonged to your parents.'

'Oh.' Charlotte looked despondent. 'If there is, it will explain what happened to them.'

'We will go after we have eaten, and then we will prepare for our trip to the mountains.'

After they had eaten, Charlotte put on her riding jacket and they went to the town hall. People pointed at Charlotte as they walked there and talked behind their hands. Charlotte became awfully self-conscious and blushed red.

They entered the main meeting room of the town hall which had portraits of all the burgers around the walls. Several tables were covered with pieces of jewellery. The gold and silver coins and the gems were not there as they could not be individually identified. Further investigation would be made to attempt to find the owners before it became the property of Harbourtown. Charlotte saw several items that had belonged to her parents, confirming that the robbers were the ones who had murdered them. One of the items was a silver brooch of an eagle. Charlotte remembered it from when she was a child and asked a sergeant of the constables if she could take it. The sergeant told her that the items of jewellery were supposed to remain there until all pieces that could be recognised were claimed. He also remembered that Charlotte had saved his daughter's life when she was suffering with a severe fever the previous winter. He put a finger to his lips and gave her the brooch which she fastened to her riding jacket. Charlotte and Sir Philip then left the town hall. Sir Philip stopped off at the armourer on the way back to Charlotte's apothecary in order to purchase a new battle axe to replace the one they buried with Dobbin. They then went to prepare for their journey.

That afternoon they provisioned themselves for the trip. They also bought some extra supplies as it was a five-day trip each way. Sir Philip joked that maybe they should hitch a ride with a couple of harpies. Charlotte did not find the joke at all funny and gave Sir Philip a not-too-friendly punch in the stomach. Towards the evening they were visited by Burger Thompson and Burger Jackson and three constables including Jim. Burger Thompson shrugged as he entered as if the following had nothing to do with him.

Burger Jackson glared at Charlotte and snarled, 'We have heard a rumour that you are planning to leave Harbourtown in the morning. Is this true?'

Sir Philip moved between Burger Jackson and Charlotte. He answered, angrily, 'That's no secret. We are going to the mountains to find a hermit in order to find out how to stop Charlotte being murdered, not that you seem to care.'

Burger Jackson raised himself to his full height and answered, 'That sounds like more illegal magic, but you are wrong, I care very much that someone accused of a serious crime that is still under investigation is leaving Harbourtown.'

Sir Philip scowled at the burger. 'Would you rather she stay here and be murdered?'

'No, you may go as she hasn't been convicted' — he left a short pause — 'yet, but you must take two constables with you to make sure that she' — he pointed at Charlotte — 'Princess Charlotte, or Charlotte Silver or whatever other name she may think up, returns. Constables Jim Stevens and David Watson,' who was of medium height and medium build with white hair, 'will go with you.'

'The more the merrier,' Sir Philip answered. 'Why don't you come too?'

'I am still investigating her crimes. I plan to be ready to charge her with them when she returns.' He pointed at the constables. 'You two stay here and go with them and make sure she comes back. I don't care what Sir Philip does.' He turned and left with the last constable.

Burger Thompson shrugged. 'Sorry, I could not stop this.'

Charlotte gave a smile. 'That's okay, Jim and David are nice people.' Jim and David smiled sheepishly. 'Did Burger Rowles and his men get back?'

'Not yet; if they are not back by tomorrow night, we will send out scouts to find them. Now I must say goodnight. Good luck on your mission.' He turned and bowed to Charlotte. 'With your leave, Princess.'

Charlotte gave a small laugh. 'Certainly, we will see you when we get back.'

Princess Scarlett had been throwing books around the queen's library in a great rage. The library was another of the castle's largest rooms. The walls were all covered with shelves of books except for the one door that led in there. The ceiling was wooden beamed with thick plates of glass between the beams for light to penetrate and the floor boasted a thick red carpet. Some of the books were now strewn on the floor or on some of the many tables in the room. She was in such a bad mood that everyone in the castle was trying to avoid her.

She was now in the laboratory where she had summoned the wraith, which now hovered in front of her. 'I want you to go to Harbourtown and find out what my sister and Sir Philip are up to and, if possible, kill her,' she ordered. 'And a warning' — she pointed to the puddle of green slime that was still on the ground — 'that is the last one that failed me.'

'I will not fail,' the wraith hissed and left through the wall.

A few minutes later the queen entered the laboratory in full regalia, screaming. 'What is going on? What did you do to my library? And what's this mess?' She looked down at the green slime and sniffed. 'Is that one of my harpies?' she added in a much quieter voice.

Princess Scarlett cringed, 'Yes, mother, I have been having some problems with ...'

'Stop!' the queen shouted, 'I don't want to know. Just

make sure you sort out the library and clean up this mess.'
She looked at the slime. 'Have I lost both of them?' she
asked apprehensively.

'Yes, mother,' Princess Scarlett answered, not looking
at her mother.

The queen glared at her forcing herself not to speak.
She turned and stormed from the room.

CHAPTER 16

Very early next morning, Charlotte, Sir Philip, Jim and David collected their horses and set off into the forest. The men were all armoured, Sir Philip in full armour except for his helmet which was on his saddle pommel, Jim and David in the breast-and-back-plate armour and helmet of Harbourtown constables, and Charlotte wearing her riding clothes. They rode north-west towards Mount Adelphi. They also led a spare horse carrying supplies and equipment. The three men were well armed as the territory they were going to pass through was wild and dangerous. 'How long to get there?' David called.

Sir Philip answered, 'Five days to get there — who

knows how long to find him — and then five days back.' David sighed.

The first day's trip was uneventful except for the masses of annoying flying insects that pestered them non-stop. They stopped and camped for the night in a clearing. The next day's travel was also uneventful. They decided to make camp early as they found a stream not too far from a clearing. Just after they made camp, a poorly dressed man walked into the clearing. Sir Philip, Jim and David all grabbed their swords immediately. The man who was tall, dark, very slender and very hairy lifted his hands. 'I have no weapon. I come to speak to Princess Charlotte.'

Charlotte, surprised, asked, 'How did you know who I was?'

'A wraith came to our pack to enlist our help to kill you. Dobbin saved my life once and we were friends. He had sworn to protect you, so I am returning my obligation to him by warning you.'

Charlotte answered, 'I thank you for your warning. What do you mean "pack"?'

'We are ten werewolves. I will not fight with them against you, so that will leave nine and one wraith who will attack.'

Sir Philip started to look around. He shouted to Jim,

'Move the fire closer to that big, dead tree and then build it up. We are going to need all the light we can get when it gets dark and then help David.' He shouted to David, 'We're going to sharpen stakes and make a rough palisade around the camp. Keep your weapons near you. What's your name?' he called to the werewolf.

'Helmut,' the werewolf replied.

'Are you on our side or neutral?'

'I will not fight against my pack.'

'I understand. Thank you for the warning. What do you get out of this'?

'Hopefully, the goodwill of the next Queen of Falconia.' He bowed towards Charlotte, who stood amazed and shaking her head. 'And to take over the pack from one who does not deserve it. I wish you luck. You will need it.' Helmut turned and left the camp.

'Four humans against nine monsters. I don't fancy our chances,' David gloomily noted.

'Ten. You forgot the wraith. Keep working. We're not dead yet,' Sir Philip answered.

Charlotte was also helping by using Sir Philip's throwing axe to cut down bushes and intertwining them into what seemed to be huge gaps between the stakes. A large branchless, dead tree protected their rear and four of the horses were tethered to it. Jenny was left free.

Finally, the sun set. The fire blazed high throwing out lots of light and heat and the companions continued to try to make their meagre palisade stronger. The men sweated profusely, having all donned their armour ready for the attack which they knew could come at any time. The half-moon rose about two hours after sunset. From out of the forest the wraith appeared followed by nine large wolves with massive heads and teeth.

David nudged Jim. 'I thought they were only supposed to turn into wolves on the full moon.'

Jim answered, 'Maybe you should go and tell them that.'

The wraith and werewolves approached the makeshift fortification and the wraith hissed, 'We meet again.'

Sir Philip raised his visor and answered, 'Yes, but why?'

'Princess Scarlett wishes her sister dead. I do not know why, just that I am going to gain great favour by accomplishing her mission. I have no grudge against you. In fact, before this, I have saved your life. Nor do I have a grudge against these two men you have with you. Give me Scarlett's sister and you may leave with your lives.'

'That sounds reasonable,' David offered.

Sir Philip, Charlotte and Jim all glared at him. 'Just a thought,' David murmured, and took a stronger grip on his sword.

Sir Philip turned to the wraith. 'We may all die, but I assure you, before I die, I will kill you.'

The wraith replied, 'I am not so easy to kill.'

Sir Philip spoke louder to make sure his companions all heard him. 'The way to kill a wraith with weapons is to stab or hit it right between the eyes; anywhere else won't hurt it.'

'None of you will get the chance,' it hissed. It turned to the wolves and pointed with its claw, 'Attack!'

The wolves moved forward slowly. Sir Philip lowered his visor. The four companions stood around the fire. Sir Philip watched the front, with the constables on the flanks. Charlotte, with Sir Philip's throwing axe, stood a little behind Jim on the left flank with the horses at the back next to the massive dead tree, its trunk about eight feet in diameter. One of the wolves bounded forward and jumped the palisade. Sir Philip met the attack with his shield and the werewolf bounced off it to impale itself on one of the stakes. It howled in agony as it slowly died. The others attacked and jumped the palisade. Two went for each of the men and one went for Charlotte and one for the horses. Sir Philip held one of his attackers at bay with his shield while the other tried to bite his head through his helmet and failed. Sir Philip hit the wolf in the jaw with his mail-clad hand which contained his sword.

The strike stunned the wolf and it fell to the ground. Sir Philip then stabbed the wolf in the throat while still holding off the other with his shield. Behind Sir Philip two wolves leapt at Jim who, backing away, tripped. The two wolves collided in mid-air and bounced away but quickly recovered. Jim was up swiftly and backed himself against the palisade while the two wolves advanced on him from either side. The two wolves that went for David had more luck. One went for his leg. That attack David was able to counter with his shield. David then went to thrust his sword into the wolf leaving his upper body open. The second wolf leapt at his throat biting down as its leap took it past David, taking David's throat with it. David died instantly, blood cascading from where his throat used to be. The werewolf that attacked the horses probably assumed that it had the easiest mission. It leapt the fence and in two bounds was leaping at the tethered horses when it received a massive kick from Jenny's two strong, iron-shod, rear hoofs. There was a loud crack and it sailed back over the palisade with several broken ribs. It staggered back towards the forest.

The last and biggest werewolf attacked Charlotte. It crashed into her knocking the throwing axe out of her hand. It stood over her; drool dripping into Charlotte's face as the teeth got closer. It was about to tear Charlotte's head off when it disappeared. Well, it seemed to Charlotte it disappeared. In fact, it was in the air above her, held by a gigantic black eagle, helpless in its claws. The eagle screeched and tore the werewolf in two. Blood and gore flew on top of all the combatants. At the sound of the screech and the rain of blood, everybody and everything stopped, frozen in place. Sir Philip recovered first. He lifted his sword and brought it down heavily, cutting the head off the second werewolf that had been attacking him. He then went to help Jim. The eagle screeched again and swooped at the werewolf that had killed David. The eagle's claws hit the wolf's torso and it was rammed into David's other attacker. They crashed together and both were bowled into the substantial fire. Both the wolves gave loud howls as their fur caught fire. They leapt back over the palisade and fled the clearing with their fur burning. The last two werewolves that had been advancing on Jim looked at each other and decided that discretion was the better part of valour and also jumped back over the palisade and fled. Sir Philip pushed himself between two of the stakes and advanced towards the wraith, his sword in his hand. The wraith, seeing the battle lost, hissed, 'Enjoy your victory, it will be your last.' It retreated and quickly faded back into the forest.

Sir Philip turned back towards the camp. It was a mess.

There were the bits of four dead werewolves scattered about the camp and on the palisade, David's dead body, and blood everywhere. The eagle, taller than Sir Philip, was standing outside the palisade cleaning blood out of its feathers. Charlotte was trying to calm the horses, all of which were terrified except for Jenny who was nuzzling the others to help Charlotte calm them. Jim was helping them. Sir Philip went and faced the giant eagle and bowed. 'Thank you for your help. We would be dead if not for you.'

The eagle looked up, gave a loud squawk and went back to cleaning its feathers. 'Interesting comment,' Sir Philip added, with a smile.

Sir Philip went back inside the palisade and helped with the horses. After they had been calmed, Sir Philip said to Jim and Charlotte, 'You two get some sleep near the tree. It's less bloody. I'll take first watch and I'll wake Jim in four-and-a-half hours for his turn.'

'Make that three hours and I'll take a turn also after Jim,' Charlotte declared.

'Are you sure?' Sir Philip asked.

'Of course, we are all trying to survive at the moment.'

'All right. Get some sleep. We'll make our plans first thing in the morning.'

Charlotte looked at the eagle outside the palisade and murmured, 'There is something I have to do first.'

She left the enclosure and walked up to the eagle. 'I have to thank you for my life. I am extremely grateful.' The eagle took a step back and bowed before her. Then it gave a loud squawk and stood still.

Charlotte patted its beak and gave it a kiss. She then returned to the camp and the tree and went to sleep. The rest of the night was uneventful.

CHAPTER 17

n the morning, after they had cleaned themselves
up, they used the small shovel that was part of their
equipment on the pack horse to dig a shallow grave
for David. They then covered it with rocks to protect it
from animals. They all said a few words over the grave
and offered David's soul to Craidos, the God of Order.
Then they started to prepare to continue their journey.

They were going to leave the werewolves' bodies
which had become human-like. There were three men
and one woman. All were naked and bore the marks of
their wounds from the previous night. One was headless,
one was still impaled on the palisade, one was torn in two
and the female had a hole in her stomach. The eagle was
still standing preening itself outside the palisade. Helmut

walked out of the forest and into the clearing and looked at the carnage. The eagle moved towards him and gave a warning squawk and Helmut stopped. Sir Philip left the camp and walked over to him. Sir Philip held out his hand and Helmut shook it. Sir Philip nodded to Helmut. 'We have to thank you for your warning, but it was almost to no avail. We lost one man and are thankful for the intervention of our friend the eagle here for our survival.'

Helmut nodded back. 'I have mixed feelings. I knew these people.' He gestured towards the bodies. 'We were one pack. We have two members with some minor burns, but they will quickly recover and one with some broken ribs who'll be inactive for a while.' He paused, then continued, 'I wish to ask a favour.'

'What? We owe you for your warning.'

'We wish to recover the bodies of our pack.'

'We will be gone in an hour at the most, you may recover them then. Is the pack leader one of them?'

'He is the one torn in two. I am the new pack leader.'

Sir Philip smiled. 'Then some good has come of this.'

The eagle started to chirrup. Helmut stopped and turned his head as if listening. Sir Philip incredulously said, 'You speak eagle?'

Helmut answered, 'I understand the eagle's chirrups. I do not need to speak it as it understands our language.'

Sir Philip gave a great sigh. 'Good, that will be a huge help. May I ask you to interpret for me?'

'Yes, on one condition.'

'What?'

'You will help collect my pack's bodies for the funeral pyres.'

'If that is the only way we can get you to interpret, then, yes, I agree.'

Sir Philip called Charlotte to join him and then told Jim to start putting the transformed bodies into a line.

Sir Philip told Charlotte that Helmut could understand the eagle's chirrups so that they could ask it questions.

Charlotte was hugely pleased with this news and started to ask the eagle questions. First, she asked the eagle where it had come from. The eagle informed them through Helmut that he had come from the eagle brooch in the same way as the dolphins had come from the bracelet. When Charlotte was in need and she was wearing the brooch or the bracelet the eagle or the dolphins would appear. She was wearing the bracelet when the sharks attacked her, so the dolphins appeared. She was wearing the brooch in the forest, so the eagle appeared. The dolphins couldn't really help in these circumstances. Her adoptive parents had created the silver items for her, to protect her from any dangers.

There was also a ring with a wolf's head upon it and a pendant in the shape of a bear, both of which had still to be found. Charlie and the other robbers must have the ring and pendant still amongst their treasure. It was only luck that the brooch had been among the loot left behind and then spotted by Charlotte.

Charlotte commented that it was probably the best piece of luck she had ever had as otherwise they would have been werewolf meat. Helmut noted that sometimes there was more than luck involved in events.

Sir Philip added that the fairy, Aengus, had said much the same thing.

The eagle, through Helmut, said it knew their mission as it could hear what they said even while it was a brooch. It knew where the hermit lived and could fly Charlotte there in less than a day. They agreed this would be a great idea except that Sir Philip did not like the idea of Charlotte going on her own. It was pointed out that the eagle would be with her and, in order to help with communication, when Charlotte asked the eagle a question, it would give one chirrup for "yes" and two for "no". They should be back within three days; much less than almost two weeks that was otherwise expected. They built a harness from leather and rope to attach to the eagle's claws for Charlotte to ride in as she was too big for the eagle's back and, besides, she would interfere with its wings for flying. They prepared provisions for her that would last for five days. They had plenty as it was believed they would need food for two weeks for four people when they set out.

It was late morning when they were ready to leave. Before Charlotte began to climb into the harness, she shouted to the eagle, 'Wait! I don't know your name.' The eagle chirruped.

Helmut translated, 'The eagle is called Great Wing.'

'What a beautiful name,' Charlotte declared. The eagle chirruped and bowed to her.

Charlotte then climbed into the harness and tied herself in. Sir Philip also attached the bag that contained her supplies and with a flap of its mighty wings the eagle rose into the air and started to fly towards the mountains. At the edge of the woods an insubstantial shape watched and then melded into the forest.

CHAPTER 18

Charlotte found the experience of flying under Great Wing the most exhilarating she had ever had. It was much better than her flight with the harpies. Instead of being terrified she was able to relax and enjoy the vista. Great Wing flew about half a mile above the forest and Charlotte could see the vast expanse of trees in all directions except where it ended at the relatively thin band of mountains called the Northern Ranges which separated The Great Forest from Concordia. As the day wore on the mountains got closer and closer and the stately peak of Mount Adelphi became evident against the smaller peaks. Charlotte felt a surge of excitement at the thought that very soon she may have the answers to her many questions.

As they neared Mount Adelphi, back in Falconia the wraith was reporting to Princess Scarlett. It told her all it had heard that morning while hiding in the forest, conveniently forgetting to mention the battle of the night before between Sir Philip, Charlotte and the Harbourtown constables and the werewolves. The princess thought to herself that she would have to look the hermit up in the queen's library. Meanwhile ...

She turned to the wraith, smiling. 'You have done well. I must thank you for this news. I have an idea. While my sister is visiting the hermit, you will kill Sir Philip and his companions and then ambush and kill her when she returns.'

The wraith hissed, 'Sir Philip knows how to kill me.'

Princess Scarlett answered, 'You will have help. There is a pack of werewolves in the area. Tell them that I order that they help you kill the men and then you all organise an ambush for when she returns. You and the werewolves should be able to easily kill three men.' Princess Scarlett didn't know one of the men was already dead.

The wraith cringed inwardly and answered, 'Not a problem, mistress. Consider it done.'

'Good, I will see you in a few days to accept your good news. Now be gone.'

The wraith left through the wall and Princess Scarlett left through the more mundane method of using a door to go to the library to do some more research.

The wraith was glad it had not mentioned that the werewolves were already beaten. It knew if it had it would now be a new puddle on the queen's laboratory floor. It now had a problem though. It had to kill Charlotte, Sir Philip and Jim without the werewolves. Who or what would it get to help do this?

Sir Philip and Jim meantime kept their word and assisted Helmut and the other werewolves who were not injured, to place their dead onto four separate funeral pyres which were built on the opposite side of the clearing to the palisade. These were then set alight and the bodies burnt. The werewolves left shortly after the pyres were set alight, not waiting for them to finish burning.

Sir Philip and Jim then started to strengthen their camp and the palisade; not that they didn't trust the werewolves, but remembering the adage, 'It's better to be safe than sorry.' Also, only one of them ever slept at a time and they always had at least one weapon near them. They made their watchwords, 'Ever Vigilant.'

It was after mid-afternoon when Great Wing and Charlotte finally left the forest behind and were flying among the mountains. Mount Adelphi stood out from the rest. It was taller than any other in the area and its snow cap seemed to cover the top quarter of the mountain. As they got closer, Charlotte saw about halfway down the mountain a wide ledge which Great Wing seemed to be heading for. As Great Wing was coming into land on the ledge Charlotte saw a cave entrance and several paths leading both up and down the mountain. Great Wing landed very carefully on the ledge to ensure Charlotte was safe. Charlotte asked, 'Is this it? Are we there?' The eagle chirruped once. 'Thank you, Great Wing.' Charlotte unattached herself and her supplies from the harness. The eagle then perched on the ledge next to her.

There was a massive echoing growl from the cave entrance and a giant, black grizzly bear came out. It was at least ten feet tall, had a massive body, long legs and very sharp claws and teeth. Charlotte backed away towards the edge of the ledge terrified. Great Wing didn't move.

A tall man wearing sheepskin clothing came out of the cave and stood next to the bear. 'It's all right, Bruno. They are friends' — he paused for a moment — 'I think.' He gave a slight bow. 'You are the Princess Charlotte, I hope, not the Princess Scarlett?' He gave Charlotte a quizzing look and put a calming hand on the bear.

'Yes,' Charlotte answered moving away from the ledge's edge. 'Are you the hermit?'

'Yes,' he answered, grinning, 'Did you expect someone else?'

'No,' Charlotte answered. 'It's just that you're not what I expected.'

'Yes, I know; everyone expects an old man with white hair and a beard down to his knees.' It was true he did not look like what people expect a hermit to look like. He was in his late thirties, six feet four inches tall, had short black hair and no beard. Instead of a long, flowing, white robe, he was wearing black sheepskin trousers and a white sheepskin jacket. At his side was a large, leather pouch. He also wore a silver pendant in the shape of a bear. He smiled. 'My name is Colin and I used to be a friend of your parents, Stephen and Julie. Well, the people you thought were your parents.'

Charlotte gasped. 'So, you're the Colin they used to talk about. You were banished from Harbourtown.'

'Yes, thanks to my friend here.' He patted the giant grizzly, 'They don't much like people who are friends with wild animals.'

Charlotte nodded. 'Yes, especially Burger Jackson; more people are changing though. I hope one day soon the laws will be changed.'

Colin gave a wry grin. 'I'm sure you did not get Great Wing there to fly you here just to talk about the unfair laws of Harbourtown.' Great Wing nodded in acknowledgement of his name. 'We have much more important things to talk about.'

Charlotte looked at Colin in surprise. 'You know Great Wing's name? How?'

'I've known Great Wing a long time. Bruno here is called Bruno.' He patted the bear again. 'The wolf is called Jason and the dolphins, Sleeky and Speedy. All beautiful animals and all jet black.'

Charlotte was taken aback. 'You know them all! Who's Jason?'

'Yes, hopefully you will meet Jason soon. He's a wolf. I helped your parents create them, but enough of this, come into my humble abode and we will discuss all that is happening.' He looked at the sun. 'The sun is almost gone, and Bruno and Great Wing will want to hunt while there is still some light.'

'They hunt?' Charlotte quizzed. 'I thought they turned back into artefacts.'

'They do,' Colin answered, 'but when they are animals, they have animal feelings and instincts, including the joy of the hunt. I like to let them enjoy themselves before they turn back.'

He led the way into the cave. 'Watch out for bats, there's quite a few I have to share the cave with.'

The entrance opened into a voluminous cavern. Charlotte could not see the roof even though white crystals around the cave gave off enough light so everything in the lower part of the cave was brightly lit. Around the walls of the cave shallow holes had been cut into the walls. Most were crammed with scrolls, books and crystals. There were crystals of all colours, even rainbow and multicoloured ones. They came in all sizes; some the size of small pebbles to one about two feet in diameter which stood on a rock near the back of the cave. Also, near the back of the cave were two passages. At the centre of the cave was a hearth where a pleasant fire was burning and on a spit over the fire a rabbit was roasting. Colin invited Charlotte to sit on one of several flat-topped rocks around the fire that were obviously used as chairs. Water was also boiling in a pot on the fire that contained an herbal tea. 'Not a lot, but we can share.'

Charlotte answered, opening her bag of provisions, 'I have lots of supplies and some chamomile tea which we can share.'

'I haven't had chamomile tea for years.' Colin smiled. 'Let's eat and drink first and then we'll talk.'

After they had eaten, Charlotte told Colin everything that had happened to her and all that Sir Philip had told her that had happened to him. Colin sat there for a while, thinking.

'Well, it's you or her,' he said, meaning Princess Scarlett. 'You are going to have to kill her.'

Charlotte looked shocked. 'I can't.'

'You'll have to or die yourself. You will have help. The animals. They were all meant for you anyway. I only got to keep Bruno because I was testing the pendant and was spotted by a constable. They wouldn't let me back into the town. Your parents let me keep him until you need him, to help me with my exile. It's a pity you haven't found Jason, but, hopefully, you may get him back before you must face Princess Scarlett. You see the broken pendant around your neck?' Charlotte nodded. 'That is magical; your sister also has one. It is the other half of that one.' Charlotte fingered the pendant. 'It used to belong to your father, but when Queen Katerina sacrificed him to Braidos and her Magic, it split in two. Both you and your sister were given half when you were born, as ordered by the "Magic".'

Charlotte interrupted, 'The "Magic"?'

Colin stroked his chin. 'How do I explain the unexplainable.' He paused. 'The "Magic" is everywhere and in everything. It is stronger in some than in others. It is what gives the gods their powers and the gods can magnify its powers in individuals. Your mother, Queen Katerina, is strong in the Magic, as are you and your sister. She made a deal with Braidos, the God of Chaos, to make herself even stronger. The deal was she would sacrifice her husband, King Edmond, to make her daughter the greatest witch who ever lived, stronger than even Katerina's mother, which would be some feat. The problem was she had twins. Queen Katerina thought she could solve her problem by sending you away with Dobbin. She couldn't kill you herself as the Magic doesn't approve of filicide.'

Charlotte interrupted, 'Filicide?'

Colin continued, 'That's when a parent deliberately kills his or her child. That's why she sent you away with Dobbin. She thought that there would be no way you would survive, and she would not have deliberately killed you. Unfortunately, the Magic doesn't seem to have any thoughts on sororicide.'

Charlotte looked blank.

'That's when a sister kills her own sister. Which is why, now that Queen Katerina and Princess Scarlett know you exist, you are in danger. Queen Katerina can do nothing openly or Braidos, the God of Chaos, will claim her and the deal is off. No restrictions on Princess Scarlett, though, and she will do anything to kill you.'

Charlotte dropped her head in her hands and then looked up appealingly. 'Is there anything I can do to stop this?'

'Queen Katerina and Princess Scarlett are strong in the Magic, especially as they are helped by Braidos.' Colin looked at Charlotte seriously. 'However, the Magic has extremely strict rules and even it is not all powerful. It can be beaten.'

Charlotte leaned forward. 'How?'

'Your father's pendant.' Colin pointed at Charlotte's half of the pendant around her neck. 'Whoever unites the pendant will have supremacy over the other sister. Unless of course one of you dies first.'

Charlotte asked, 'How do you know all this?'

'Most I have learnt using the crystal over there.' He gestured to the large crystal on the rock column. 'You will need to unite the halves to beat your sister.'

'So, I'm to get it from around her neck. How?'

'She does not wear it. I don't know why. I visited Falconia once and saw her. She was wearing a low cut, very immodest top, which I'm sure all the local lads noticed, and she was wearing no pendants at all. So, all you need to do is get into her rooms, find her half of the pendant and join them together and, presto, you win.'

'That's all. Sounds easy,' Charlotte said, sarcastically.

'I'm sure you'll have no problem.' Colin smiled. 'I think you'll need to study your mother's journals while you travel to Falconia. I have copies of most of them here. That is extremely important. Your mother had powers that could help you; and if the worst comes to the worst you can always cut off Princess Scarlett's head.'

Charlotte looked shocked and shook her head. 'I could never do that. Why am I just learning all this?'

Colin answered, 'The queen, your real mother, has just found out you are still alive. She had hoped you had died when Dobbin took you away and did not return to her. As I said, the queen can take no action against you herself, or help to attack you, without destroying herself. Princess Scarlett is destined to become the most powerful witch who as ever lived, but at the moment she is a bungler. You must kill her now before she gets stronger and more competent.'

Charlotte just sat there shaking her head.

'Your mother's journals are hidden in a secret panel behind the headboard of your parents' bed, but as I said, I have copies of most of them. You must read them. You have powers of your own; you must learn to use them. Now you must get some sleep. We must return to your friends early tomorrow. The sooner you kill Princess Scarlett the better.'

'I don't think I can,' Charlotte answered, with tears in her eyes.

'Then prepare to die.'

Colin got up and went to one of the holes in the wall and pulled out some blankets. He gave Charlotte several and kept some for himself. 'We will talk more in the morning. Good night, Princess Charlotte.'

Charlotte smiled through her tears. 'Goodnight, Colin.'

As they lay down to go to sleep, they didn't see a bat fluttering out of the front of the cave.

CHAPTER 19

The next morning just before dawn the queen was woken up by a strange noise at one of her bedroom windows. She climbed out of the large, four-poster bed and, clad only in her nightdress, went to the window. A bat was flapping its wings against the window. The queen recognised it at once and let it in. It was the bat she had sent many years ago to spy on the hermit at Mount Adelphi and then forgotten about. The bat had never reported back to her as it never had anything to report. Now it had. The bat screeched to her the gist of the meeting between Charlotte and Colin. The queen now knew that Princess Scarlett was under threat. She conjured a large rat out of thin air and gave it to the bat for a reward. She dressed and then went to speak to her daughter, Princess Scarlett.

The wraith meanwhile had gone to speak to the werewolves to see if it could persuade them into a second attack. They weren't interested, especially as Sir Philip and Jim had helped cremate the dead members of the pack and Helmut ordered it to leave their camp and never return. The wraith went to the edge of the forest and watched Sir Philip and Jim working on the palisade and wondered what it should do. It decided it would seek the help of a pair of redcap goblins it knew that lived not too far away. Redcap goblins did not like humans at the best of times.

Sir Philip and Jim had spent the previous day helping the werewolves burn their dead on the four separate funeral pyres and strengthening the camp against possible attack. The palisade now was almost complete and there was only a narrow-barred gate just large enough to lead a horse through. They kept their weapons close at hand even though they did not wear their full armour, as it was impossible to wear all of it and work on the palisade, Sir Philip only wore his breast and back plates and Jim just his leather jerkin. Only one of them slept or ate at a time.

At the cave on Mount Adelphi Charlotte was getting ready to leave. Colin was talking to Great Wing. Charlotte shook her head. 'I wish I could talk to Great Wing the way you do, instead of two chirrups for "no" and one chirrup for "yes".'

'I am able to talk to all of the Silvers' animals. I tested the bracelet, the pendant, the ring and the brooch. As I said before, I was testing the pendant when I was spotted by people at Harbourtown and exiled. I have been thinking. After Great Wing returns you to Sir Philip, send him back and I will come out to you and help you. You may need my extra help.'

'It could take up to two days for you to catch up with us if we start to head towards Falconia. How will you find us?'

Colin handed her a small, blue crystal. 'Carry this and I will find you. I won't take long to find you because I'll be flown by Great Wing. You had better take this too.' He gave her the bear pendant. 'Your parents meant for you to have it. Also, these' — he gave her two large books — 'copies of your mother's journals.'

Charlotte gave him a kiss on the cheek. 'Thank you.' She fastened herself into the harness attached to Great Wing. 'See you soon.' Great Wing took off and headed back to her friends' camp.

At the camp, Sir Philip and Jim had just had a cold breakfast of oatmeal. Sir Philip had not yet donned any of his armour after sleeping, Jim having the second watch. Jim told Sir Philip he would just go down to the stream and get some water to brew some tea. He picked up a tin bucket and left. The stream was about fifty yards away and Sir Philip started to get worried when Jim had not returned after ten minutes. He picked up his sword and shield and started to leave the palisade.

'So, we meet again.' It was the red-headed Charlie the Mean. He had three large, burly men dressed in green with him, all better armed than the men whom he had fought at Dobbin's camp. All had swords and Charlie also carried an axe. Two of them were holding the tied, gagged and struggling Jim. 'Surrender, and we will let the constable live.'

Sir Philip replied, 'If I surrender you will kill us both. Release the constable and I will let you live.'

Charlie laughed. 'You've no monsters to help you this time. I warned you.' He turned and nodded to his men. One produced a long-bladed knife and proceeded to slowly cut Jim's throat, but paused as Sir Philip screamed at Charlie, 'No, wait!'

Charlie turned and smiled. 'Too late.' He nodded to the man with the knife who continued with his task. Blood flowed into the clearing in front of the palisade. 'Get logs to use as steps to get over the wall,' Charlie ordered his men. 'Put some on both sides. He can't be in two places at once.'

His men went to get logs. There were plenty about as Sir Philip and the constables had left logs that they had rejected for the palisade just lying about. Charlie snarled at Sir Philip, 'You have caused me a lot of grief. I've lost my camp and most of my men. Fortunately, I still have most of my treasure. However, you will be punished. We are going to take you alive and you will take a long time to die.'

Sir Philip gave a laugh he did not really feel. Even a warrior like him was shocked at the cold, callous way Jim had been murdered. 'You talk well and fight like a limp fish. It shouldn't take long to dispose of you and your men. I hope you live. I would just love to see you hung, drawn and quartered.'

In fact, Sir Philip was worried. He knew he could defend one part of the wall against them, but while he was doing so the other side would be undefended and whoever came over it would be behind him. Even Jenny would be vulnerable to a well-placed sword thrust. He decided that his best option would be to defend whichever side that Charlie was on and kill him before he died himself.

Charlie's men rolled logs against the palisade and soon it was obvious that they would be able to climb it with ease. While they were doing this, Sir Philip donned his breast and back plates of his armour. He didn't have time for the rest. The robbers spread out so that it would be impossible for Sir Philip to defend all the sides and began to advance. Sir Philip moved to the right section of the palisade where he could protect it best from Charlie and one of his men who was with him. Charlie and the man slowed down as they saw Sir Philip on their side while the others started to climb the logs on the opposite side. Jenny moved to the left side to watch the men and they started to swing their swords to keep her at bay.

Suddenly, there was a loud howl and three large wolves bounded out of the forest. One went for each of Charlie's men who were taken completely by surprise. The two that had been threatening Jenny had just started to turn when they had their throats torn out. The third had more time and his sword thrust dug into the wolf's upper left leg. The wolf fell back standing its ground on three legs, snarling at the thug. Charlie turned and raised his axe to chop down on the injured wolf. His arm shook as Sir Philip's sword stroke took the head off the axe, leaving Charlie holding a stick. Charlie drew his sword and attacked Sir Philip across the top of the four-foot palisade. The two uninjured wolves went to their injured pack mate's aid. One attacked the man low and the other high, leaving the man undecided about which wolf to stab. The wolf that went low sank its teeth in the man's thigh while the other took his sword arm. The man dropped his sword and the wolves savaged the man's torso. He screamed loudly for a few seconds and then went quiet. The wolves then slowly advanced on Charlie who had stopped attacking Sir Philip and was holding his sword low with his back to the fence.

Sir Philip was as surprised as the robbers had been at the sudden turn of events. He watched as he was rescued by the werewolves and then he saved one wolf from Charlie, but now just as it looked as if Charlie was about to die the same way as his men, he shouted, 'Stop! That one is mine.'

The wolves stopped and watched as Sir Philip

unbarred the narrow gate of the palisade and came into the clearing. Charlie shook his head. 'Saved by bloody monsters again. I just don't believe it.' He threw down his sword. 'I yield.'

Sir Philip advanced on Charlie. 'Unfortunately, I don't have time to take you back to Harbourtown where you should be tried, so I will take care of you here and now myself.'

Charlie looked around for a means of escape, but there was none. The wolves surrounded him. Even the one with the wounded leg would be able to catch him. 'I have yielded. I demand a trial,' he shouted.

Sir Philip took a step forward and snarled, 'Pick up your weapon, you gutless coward, or I will give you to the wolves.'

Charlie fell to his knees and clasped his hands together, 'You couldn't be so cruel and inhumane. You are a knight.'

'Watch me. Helmut.' He waved his sword towards Charlie and one of the wolves advanced slowly towards him.

Charlie grabbed his sword and rose to face Sir Philip. 'Okay, if that's the way you want it. Call off your monster.'

Sir Philip called to Helmut, 'That's enough. This swine is mine.'

Helmut and the two other wolves slowly transformed

into humans. Two men and one woman. All were naked. The woman had a sword wound to her arm. The other male werewolf tore the shirt from one of the dead robbers and tended her arm. Helmut just stood there watching.

Charlie shook his head. 'Werewolves! Werewolves, wraiths and horse monsters. Can you win a fight without supernatural help?'

'Let's find out. This is just you and me, to make it fair.' Sir Philip threw down his shield. He also removed his front and back plates. It was sword against sword. Sir Philip advanced on Charlie. Charlie screamed a battle cry and charged towards Sir Philip, the sword swinging in a side stroke that, if it had connected, would have chopped Sir Philip's arm off. Sir Philip jumped back, and the blow cut his shirt but not his skin. He then thrust his sword forward and Charlie only just managed to knock the thrust aside. Charlie slowly retreated towards the forest realising that he could not win a fair fight against a trained knight. Helmut transformed himself back into a wolf and growled at Charlie as he placed himself between Charlie and the forest.

'No escape this time, Charlie,' Sir Philip uttered quietly. 'This time you die.'

Sir Philip advanced on his opponent, swinging his sword slowly side to side. Charlie again fell to his knees and held his arms wide. 'For the love of Craidos, this isn't a fight, this is murder.'

Sir Philip hesitated and lowered his sword to his side, Charlie was up in a flash swinging his sword to cut across Sir Philip's chest. Sir Philip had expected some sort of trick from Charlie, so he easily parried the slash and then thrust his sword towards Charlie. The thrust hit Charlie to the left of his stomach. Charlie screamed and turned and chopped down with his sword, just missing Sir Philip's head, but slicing down his arm. Sir Philip gave out a loud gasp and fell to his knees as a slice of his arm hung loose but did not drop his sword. Charlie raised his sword for a killing blow, but Sir Philip slashed him in the knee, half chopping Charlie's leg off. Charlie fell screaming in pain and dropped his sword. He lay on his back whimpering. Sir Philip used his sword to help himself regain his feet and stood over Charlie. 'This is for all your crimes. It is a much more merciful death than you deserve.'

As Sir Philip went to place his sword over Charlie's heart, Charlie pulled a small knife from a sheath on his ankle and gave Sir Philip a slight wound to his shin. Sir Philip kicked the knife away. He again placed the tip of his sword over Charlie's heart and this time pressed down hard. Charlie screamed once and silence returned to the forest.

Helmut went up to Sir Philip. 'You are hurt.' Sir Philip looked at his arm. A great slice had been cut into it and it hung nastily. We will bind it for you, but there is not much else we can do. We cannot look for your medicines as the horses belonging to these men that are down near the river will not let us approach and, also, your horses we cannot approach as they do not like our kind.'

Sir Philip grimaced painfully. 'Thank you, I owe you my life twice now. If I can ever help in any way, just ask.'

'Can you stop men from hunting us? No.' Helmut answered his own question. 'We wish you well, but you may die yet. We will also bury your man next to the other grave. You helped with our dead. We will help with yours.'

Sir Philip nodded his thanks. The werewolves bound up Sir Philip's arm with the shirts of the dead bandits and put a much smaller cloth on his leg and helped him to the open gate of the palisade, which they did not enter because of the horses. Philip left the gate open and went to sit with his back against the dead tree. The male werewolves then buried Jim. They left with the wounded woman and each carried two dead robbers, not saying what they were going to do with them, leaving Sir Philip hoping that Charlotte would not be long in returning.

CHAPTER 20

While the fight with Charlie was happening, the queen had Princess Scarlett roused from her sleep by her servants with the command that she go straight to the library to speak to her. She then went there to wait, together with her spy, the bat. Princess Scarlett had not slept well and was in a foul mood when she got to the library still in her nightdress. The queen's mood was even more foul. 'What the hell is going on!' she screamed at Princess Scarlett. 'I've just received a report that your sister is talking to the Hermit of Mount Adelphi and he has passed some very helpful information. To her, that is. She now knows how to destroy you.'

Princess Scarlett went white with shock. 'How? Surely, that is impossible.'

'No, it's possible. What happened to the half-pendant that looks like it has a half star and moon on it?' the queen asked.

Princess Scarlett's face contorted with thought. 'I don't know. I haven't seen it for years. I don't really remember it or having it since I was a child.'

'You had better find it and when you do, do NOT' — the queen emphasised the word "not" — 'let it out of your sight. Now be gone and do something right for once. I will leave you this bat to take messages.' The princess and the bat left to go Princess Scarlett's rooms where she quickly dressed and then went to the queen's laboratory.

While walking to her rooms and then the laboratory, the princess got the story from the bat of what had happened in the cave. She was livid when she heard of how the wraith had deceived her by not telling her it had already used the werewolves to attack her sister; and even worse failed to kill her. She ordered the bat to go and get the wraith immediately. 'And tell it, if it doesn't come the second it receives this order, I will destroy it in the worst way I can possibly devise!'

The bat left, leaving the princess in the laboratory. She did not know what to do. Finally, she decided to go back to her rooms to look for the medallion, not knowing where to look first. She ordered her maids to help.

The wraith had returned to the edge of the forest. The redcap goblins had refused to help it. The odds of three to two were not great enough in their minds to ensure victory, especially as they were only three feet tall. Fortunately for Sir Philip, they did not know that there was only him left and that he was badly wounded. The wraith saw no movement around the camp, Sir Philip having decided the best place for him was to stay inside the palisade. The wraith waited and watched for almost two hours without seeing movement. It glided up to the palisade and looked through a gap in the logs. It saw Sir Philip lying with his back against the tree dozing with his sword in his hand. The wraith hesitated and thought this might be its best chance of finally killing Sir Philip. It was just about to enter the fortification when a bat screeched behind it. The wraith halted, Sir Philip immediately became wide awake and alert. The wraith gave the bat a murderous look and stretched its claw towards it to tear its heart out. The bat chittered loudly at the wraith. The wraith halted and hissed a snarl and then left with the bat.

As the day progressed, Sir Philip felt himself getting weaker and weaker. His armed ached badly, but his leg felt as if it was on fire. He could barely stand the pain and was finding it hard to stay conscious. Suddenly, there was a loud flapping of wings and Great Wing and Charlotte landed just outside the palisade. Charlotte called to both Sir Philip and Jim. She did not know that Jim was dead. Sir Philip tried to call out, but all he could manage was a moan. Charlotte heard it and went to the opening in the palisade. She saw Sir Philip and gave a small cry and rushed through the narrow entrance. She rushed up to Sir Philip and started to unwrap the cloths on his arm to examine it. She cried, 'What happened? Where's Jim?'

Sir Philip answered weakly, 'Jim's dead.'

A tear formed in Charlotte's eye as she studied Sir Philip's wound. 'Stay still, I will get some herbs and medicines from my pack on Maria. While she was getting the herbs, she shouted to Great Wing, 'Go get Colin as fast as possible. He may know some magic that could help.' The great eagle stretched his wings and took off, heading for Mount Adelphi.

Charlotte built up what was left of the fire and left Bruno, who had reappeared and was guarding the camp and the entrance to the palisade. She then went to fetch water from the stream using a metal pot as the bucket was nowhere to be seen. When she got to the stream, she found the bucket already full. She heard the whinnying of a horse. She walked towards the sound. There were six of them all tied to trees. Four were saddled and had bulging saddle bags. Two had been used as pack horses and had large bags tied to them. They all looked tired and thirsty. They were the robbers' horses. Charlotte untied them and they all raced to the stream for a drink. She told them, 'Stay here, I will look after you later.' When she got back, she started to mix herbs and boil them. She also prepared a poultice. Sir Philip called to her, 'My leg, please check my left leg.'

Charlotte frowned as she tore away Sir Philip's leggings. The small wound had swollen and turned purple. 'Poison,' she muttered. She pulled another packet from her medical pack and added its contents to the herb water mix that had just started to boil. She spread most of the poultice on Sir Philip's large wound and then rebound it with fresh bandages from her pack. She then poured the boiling water into a tin cup which she held to Sir Philip's lips. It was a mix that would help Sir Philip to sleep and start healing his body, the extra additive she hoped would counteract whatever poison had been on Charlie's knife. She used what was left of the poultice on Sir Philip's small leg wound hoping that it would help draw out the poison. After she had bandaged it, she placed her hands on the wound and thought to herself, *Well, let's see how much power I really have*, and her brow wrinkled in concentration.

After about fifteen minutes she made herself some food and tea. She then went and refilled the bucket so there was water for the horses and made sure they had feed. She sat and rested herself next to Sir Philip and, as she did so, noticed the chain that she had given him. It had slipped from under his shirt so that it could be seen. It no longer held a silver rose but a lump of blackened metal. She thought this strange as she knew Sir Philip was wearing the rose pendant when they left Harbourtown. She fell asleep holding him in her arms, hoping that Great Wing and Colin would not take long, leaving Bruno guarding the camp from outside the palisade, as the horses inside seemed to feel rather uneasy having him around.

The wraith and the bat arrived at Falconia Castle. They found Princess Scarlett and her maids tearing her rooms apart. The princess was screaming at her maids for not searching well enough. As the bat and the wraith entered, the maids took one look at them and fled the room. The wraith immediately prostrated itself. 'Princess, please I beg you, give me another chance to serve you. I will not fail.'

The princess looked down at it with scorn and was about to slowly dissipate it very painfully when she thought that if she did, she would have nobody to go after her sister. Instead, she uttered to the wraith, 'Give me one good reason to let you live; that is, if you call what you do living.'

'I will kill your sister, mistress. Sir Philip is already almost dead. If you had not summoned me, I would have finished him, but no matter, he cannot last long anyway. I did try to get some redcap goblins to help me, but they refused.'

'Redcap goblins?' The princess rubbed her chin. 'Wait here.' She went to her mother's Throne Room where the queen was holding court. There were many people there, some were petitioners hoping to get decisions made in their favour, others were her courtiers. A line of guards kept them all back until it was their turn to approach the throne. The Royal Chamberlain, Sir John Amberleigh, held a list of the petitions and stood next to the throne. Two of her subjects, both rich landowners dressed in their best finery, were arguing about who owned a plot of land just outside the town wall. When the princess entered the Throne Room, the crowd parted to let her through and the guards stood aside to let her approach the queen. The queen saw the princess and shook her head slowly, as in despair. The princess curtsied to the queen. 'I have urgent business, mother.' The queen waved a dismissive hand. 'I must settle this first.' She looked down at her two subjects. 'I find that you are both at fault. Because of this I proclaim that the property belongs to the crown. Any objections?'

One of the petitioners started to protest. The queen shouted, 'Guards, throw him in the moat.' Two guards grabbed the man and dragged him from the Throne Room kicking and screaming. The queen looked at the other petitioner. 'Do you have anything to say?'

The petitioner, visibly shaking, murmured quietly, 'No, gracious queen, a very fair decision,' and backed out of the Throne Room. The queen looked around at the other petitioners, her courtiers and guards. 'Leave us. I would like to talk to my daughter and have my evening meal prepared so I may eat in half an hour.' Everyone left except Princess Scarlett. Queen Katerina glared at her daughter and sighed. 'I hope this is not more bad news. Have you found your medallion yet?'

'No, mother, but it will be found soon,' the princess answered. 'May I borrow your signet ring?'

The queen's eyed widened. 'You know that this is the Great Ring of Falconia?'

'Yes, mother. I need it because ...'

'Stop!' The queen raised a hand. 'I don't want to know.' The queen spent some time thinking. She then took off the ring and handed it down to Princess Scarlett. 'You had better look after it better than you did the medallion. It has great power.' The queen then left the Throne Room through the curtains at the back of the dais, heading for her dinner. Princess Scarlett looked longingly at the gold ring in her hand with the crown symbol of Falconia on it. She had never held it before. The ring of great authority and power.

Princess Scarlett returned to her rooms where the wraith was still prostrate on the floor and the bat was still fluttering around. She spoke first to the bat as she did not want what she was going to do reported back to the queen. 'You are ordered to go back to your spying and report anything of importance back to the queen immediately.' The bat flew up out of a window.

Princess Scarlett then turned to the wraith. 'Get up.' The wraith rose from the floor. She handed the Great Ring of Falconia to the wraith. 'Here is the Great Ring of Falconia. Take it and show it to the redcap goblins. They will not dare refuse to help you. When next I see you, I want only good news.'

The wraith replied, 'You shall have it, mistress,' and glided out through the wall.

CHAPTER 21

Charlotte woke several times during the night to tend Sir Philip when he cried out in pain. Bruno guarded the camp all night, occasionally looking over the palisade to make sure Charlotte was safe. This was not appreciated by the horses. The next morning, Sir Philip seemed slightly better and he was coherent. He told Charlotte all that had happened since she left with Great Wing. Charlotte surprised herself for feeling glad that Charlie the Mean and all his cohorts were dead. She didn't even care about what happened to their bodies. Colin and Great Wing had still not arrived. Charlotte prepared more herbal teas and medicines for Sir Philip to drink and then put a fresh poultice and bandage on his arm and leg. The arm was looking much better, but the leg was still a nasty purple, but the colour had not spread. She spent another fifteen minutes with her hands on the wound concentrating on it to get better. She then prepared a breakfast of porridge and honey which she spooned into his mouth before eating some herself. She left Sir Philip sleeping and Bruno guarding the camp while she went to the stream to fetch more water.

While she was getting the water, Charlotte checked on the robbers' horses. They were all still there. She went and gave each of them a hug and told them how good they were. She then removed the saddles and all the bags from their backs. This took her a lot of effort as the saddles, and especially the bags, were very heavy. Most she just left where they fell. She was strangely attracted to one of the saddle bags. She opened it and poured out the contents. It was full of gold coins and jewels. A ring seemed to glint at her. She stared at it and then picked it up. It was a silver ring and had a wolf's head emblazoned on it. She had seen it before, many years ago, just before her parents left on that fateful trip to Thrackstown. It was her parents' ring that they had made for her. It and the eagle brooch were going to be two of the samples they were going to show at a silver exhibition there. She put it on, and nothing happened. She thought, *Oh well, at least I now have all four of the pieces, the bracelet, the brooch, the pendant and now the ring.* She could now face her sister with a chance not to die. There was a commotion at the camp and she ran back. It was Great Wing and Colin. She ran up to Colin as he was releasing himself from the harness. 'You must help Sir Philip quickly. He is badly wounded.'

Colin answered, 'I will see what I can do,' and he entered the palisade to help Sir Philip. Charlotte went and gave Great Wing a hug, 'Thank you, Great Wing. You have been a tower of strength.' The eagle nodded its head, nuzzled her brooch and disappeared. Its disappearance made Charlotte jump. She then patted Bruno. 'Thank you too, Bruno,' and went to join Colin and Sir Philip.

Colin had placed a green crystal on each of the sleeping Sir Philip's wounds. The crystals were glowing. 'You did an excellent job with the poultice. You have saved his arm,' Colin said, looking at Charlotte. 'The crystal will finish the mending of the wound. I'm a lot more concerned about his leg. He should be dead as he has been poisoned by what I think is the venom of a southern desert viper. I don't know what kept him alive, unless it was this.' He held up the chain with the black lump to show Charlotte.'

'I think that may have been a silver rose pendant that my parents made,' Charlotte told him.

Colin nodded. 'Yes, it must have been this. It used up all its power to stop the poison from spreading. With its power gone, it was destroyed. As you have seen, your parents had some great abilities when working with silver.'

Charlotte looked anxious. 'So, he'll be alright?'

Colin nodded. 'Yes, I think so. The poison, as I said, was held where it entered and didn't spread through his body. Your ministrations, and now the crystals, should clear the poison out completely. As long as he takes it easy for the next few days, he'll be as good as new. I'll fasten the crystals to the wounds to help them heal faster.'

Charlotte breathed a sigh of relief. 'That is excellent news and, what's more, look at this.' She held up her hand to show the silver wolf's head ring.'

'That's marvellous news,' Colin exclaimed. 'You should now be strong enough to take on your sister.'

Colin was still bandaging the crystals over Sir Philip's arm and leg when loud noises started to emanate from the forest. Charlotte ran to the wall and looked over it. Charlotte saw a man on the edge of the forest in the black uniform of the Constables of Harbourtown. Bruno was starting to move towards him. Charlotte called out, 'Bruno, come here quickly.' Bruno stopped and looked back at Charlotte. 'Quick, here, now.' Bruno ambled up to Charlotte who quickly touched the pendant to Bruno's nose. Bruno disappeared. A few seconds later a

Harbourtown constable had come completely out of the forest, followed closely by Burger Rowles and the rest of his men leading their horses. Charlotte gave a squeal of delight and ran and gave Burger Rowles a big hug.

Burger Rowles who, like his men, looked rather dishevelled, looked at Charlotte and smiled. 'Fancy finding you here. What's going on?'

Charlotte replied, 'Sir Philip is badly wounded. The robbers are all dead. Unfortunately, so are Jim and David.'

'You are the only one unhurt?' Burger Rowles asked.

'No, there is another with us called Colin. He is helping Sir Philip now.'

Colin left the palisade to join them. He had left the green crystals attached to Sir Philip's arm and leg with bandages.

Burger Rowles stared at Colin. 'Don't I recognise you?' His brow furrowed in thought. 'I know, you were exiled from Harbourtown for consorting with monsters, an er ... giant bear, if I remember correctly. You're lucky we aren't in Harbourtown. You would be arrested.'

One of the constables declared, 'When I first started to enter the clearing, I thought I saw a bear.'

Burger Rowles looked around and asked the constable, 'And where is it now?'

The constable shrugged. Burger Rowles laughed. 'Must

have vanished into thin air. Poof!' He smiled. 'What happened with the robbers?'

Charlotte answered, 'There was a fight. They all got killed. Their horses are by the stream together with all their loot.' Burger Rowles pointed to four of his men. 'Go get the horses and the loot.' He turned back to Charlotte. 'Where are the bodies?'

Charlotte answered, 'David and Jim are buried over there,' and pointed to the graves at the edge of the clearing. 'We left the robbers for the animals and the bodies are gone.'

Burger Rowles pointed to the other four of his men 'Dig them up. We will take them back to Harbourtown for a proper burial.'

Only the burger and his sergeant were left with Charlotte and Colin. The burger told his sergeant, 'Go and check on Sir Philip.' The sergeant left. He turned to Charlotte, 'I am one of your godparents. I've known you since you were a baby. You're not telling the complete truth. What's happening?'

Charlotte blushed. 'It's a very long story. It will have to wait. Suffice to say we need to get to Falconia Castle as soon as possible.'

Burger Rowles stood for a couple of minutes in thought. He was interrupted by the return of his men with the horses. One shouted, 'We've got them, sir. One of the bags was open and the loot a bit scattered, but we collected it all up.' The burger thought *And some of it collected into your pockets, no doubt,* but he said nothing. One of the men leading the horses stopped and looked at the ground and bent to pick something up.

Colin shouted, 'Stop!' and moved next to the constable as he straightened. They both looked down at the small knife. Colin knelt beside it. 'That thing is covered in poison. I don't advise touching it.'

The constable stepped back. Colin pulled a set of pincers from his pack and picked up the knife. He walked over to Burger Rowles and showed him the knife. 'You see the rivulet marks on the knife? That's poison. I think we should bury this.'

Burger Rowles nodded in agreement. Colin walked to the edge of the clearing and dug a small hole under a tree with his own knife and buried the poisoned knife. 'May you never be found,' he murmured and then returned to the others.

The men who had been sent to dig up the bodies reported to Burger Rowles, 'Jim had his throat cut and David actually had his throat torn out.'

Burger Rowles turned to Charlotte and raised his eyebrows. Charlotte looked down and said, 'The robbers did not fight fair.'

The sergeant returned. 'They look like they're bad wounds, but are well bandaged. Sir Philip seems to be recovering.'

Burger Rowles told the sergeant, 'In the morning you and four of the men will take the bodies of Jim and David and most of the treasure back to Harbourtown. The other four will accompany me to escort Princess Charlotte and her companions back to her kingdom.' He turned to Charlotte and bowed. 'At your service, Princess.'

Charlotte turned to him and smiled. 'Thank you.'

CHAPTER 22

The wraith was now feeling much more confident of getting the redcap goblins to assist with its mission It had returned to the old and gnarled tree where the two redcap goblins it had spoken to before lived. Goblins are about three feet tall, have large heads and eyes and extra wide mouths with sharpened teeth; they are also yellow. There are several tribes of goblins, with each tribe wearing different coloured clothing. The redcap goblins were called Lickspit and Flatnose (you may guess how they got their names). Both wore red overalls, red caps and large red boots. Lickspit nudged Flatnose as they watched the wraith approach their tree, and whispered, 'It's that wraith who is stupid enough to want us to attack humans.'

Flatnose replied, with a chuckle, 'I wonder what wraith tastes like? Maybe smoked pork? Yum'.

The wraith reached the goblins and raised itself to its full height. It spoke with its most authoritarian hiss, 'Keep still, you spawn of swine and slime. I have the Great Ring of Falconia' — it held up its claw that was holding the ring — 'which the mighty Queen of Falconia has given me! You WILL obey me, and through me, the queen!'

The redcap goblins' eyes bulged as they looked at the ring in astonishment and then both threw themselves flat on the ground. Lickspit murmured with his mouth in the mud, 'Please forgive us, how may we serve the great queen?'

The wraith looked down with a feeling of superiority on the redcap goblins. It hesitated just for the feeling, then hissed, 'You ARE going to obey me. You ARE going to attack humans. This is the great queen's order. Go!' It pointed with its claw. 'Get all the redcap goblins that you can find. Meet me here at this tree at this time in two days with as many redcap goblins as you can find. Make sure they are ready to kill. Now, go! Hurry!'

The redcap goblins scrambled to their feet. 'Yes, master, yes, lord.' They both ran off in separate directions. The wraith waited.

The next morning found Sir Philip greatly improved. He was still weak, but the large flap of skin on his arm was knitting nicely with the rest of his arm and the purple swelling on his leg had reduced significantly in size. The sergeant and the four men he was taking back to Harbourtown tied Jim's and David's bodies to two separate horses and collected the horses that were carrying the robbers' loot. Burger Rowles had taken a bag of silver coins from the loot in case it should become necessary for his group's travels. The sergeant's group also took the spare horses and waved goodbye as they set off to Harbourtown. They made quite a procession.

The other group comprising Charlotte, Sir Philip, Colin, Burger Rowles, the other four constables and one packhorse headed into the deep forest towards Falconia.

Burger Rowles led the group with Colin bringing up the rear. Sir Philip was still recovering from his wounds so they tied him to Jenny so that he could sleep while riding safely. As they headed down a path that headed in a westerly direction, the forest got thicker and darker. Eventually, the path disappeared altogether.

Burger Rowles ordered two of his constables to hack a path with their swords through the forest that could be followed. Everyone except Sir Philip dismounted and led their horses. The pack horse was tied to Jenny so she could look after it. The forest was eerily dark and spooky. Even though it was midday, almost no sunlight got through the forest's thick canopy of leaves. There were strange noises and growls coming from every direction, even above and, one of the constables thought, below. Insects were attacking them from all directions and all of them were covered in bites except Charlotte and Colin. At about mid-afternoon they came upon an animal track which headed in a westerly direction. They all remounted. One of the constables who had been chopping through the forest commented to another, 'Well, this should make things a bit easier.' The other replied, 'True, unless we come across whatever made this track.'

About an hour before dark, they came across a small clearing. Burger Rowles called a halt. 'We will camp here for the night. I hope we won't all be eaten alive by then. These insects are murder.'

Colin smiled. 'I will set up a perimeter that insects and other creatures will find difficult to cross. You will have an insect-free night, from those outside the perimeter, at least.' Colin dismounted and started to look around the clearing inspecting the tree branches. The others, except for Sir Philip, had also dismounted and were watching

Colin with bemusement. Colin found a straight branch. 'Burger Rowles, could you please get one of your men to cut this branch, so it becomes a staff?'

Burger Rowles turned to his men. 'Morris, you heard him. Get moving.'

'Oh and start collecting wood for a fire. It will be very difficult later.'

'You other three, get to it,' Burger Rowles ordered.

One of the constables moved towards Colin, unsheathing his sword as he did so, while the others started to collect firewood. He reached the branch and started hacking at it. While he was doing this, Charlotte and Burger Rowles helped Sir Philip from Jenny and made sure he was sitting comfortably against a log. A few minutes later, Morris had finished and handed a six-foot staff to Colin. Colin moved to the centre of the clearing and rammed one end of the staff into the ground. He took from his bag a large, yellow crystal, which he placed on top of the staff. It stayed there without adhesive. He then took a handful of smaller yellow crystals from his bag and walked around the outside of the clearing placing the smaller yellow crystals no further than three yards from each other. When he had completely placed crystals all around the clearing, he went back to the staff and waited until the constables had accumulated a sizeable pile of firewood. He then placed both hands on the large crystal and whispered a few words. A yellow mist fountained above the staff and spread until all the small crystals were reached and then stopped, leaving an opaque, yellow, dome-shaped screen around the camp.

Burger Rowles drew his sword, pointed it at Colin and scowled. 'Magic! Constables, arrest this man at once.'

Charlotte screamed out, 'Stop, what are you doing?' and jumped in front of Colin. The constables hesitated.

Colin stepped forward next to Charlotte. 'I think you'll find we are now in Falconia, which makes Princess Charlotte the authority here.' He bowed to her. 'What is your wish, Your Highness?'

Charlotte turned to Burger Rowles who had waved to his men to stop. She said, 'Colin, please explain to me and the others what you have done.'

'Certainly, Princess.' He spread his hands. 'What you see will not only keep the insects at bay but will also help to protect us from every other creature in the forest. Anything that moves through the border of the screen will be slowed down to about a tenth of its speed. Insects will die. Larger creatures may or may not but will probably avoid it anyway. Large or hostile creatures we will be able to kill before they are completely inside. The screen will make us safe.'

Burger Rowles rubbed his chin. 'Well, as we are in Falconia and not in Harbourtown territory, I suppose Harbourtown laws don't apply. I don't advise you return there, though.'

They built a small fire and ate a supper of stale bread and cheese. After supper, Burger Rowles, Charlotte, Colin, and Sir Philip who was still propped up next to a log, sat in a quiet spot away from the constables. Sir Philip was recovering faster than anyone had expected. Colin had left his green crystals tied to Sir Philip's wounds.

'Well,' Burger Rowles asked, 'What's all this about? I must say I'm a bit concerned about this use of magic.'

Charlotte shook her head. 'I'm afraid that you'll have to get used to it now we're in Falconia.' She told him the whole story, including the parts about the bracelet, pendants, brooch and ring. By the time she had finished, the sun had gone down, but the yellow screen still emitted a dim light in the clearing.

'It's fortunate that you are a Princess of Falconia. I don't think you will be welcome in Harbourtown unless we change the laws.'

Charlotte replied, 'When I have settled whatever is going to happen in Falconia, I am going to improve ties with Harbourtown and I will try to get the law and the prejudices overturned.'

'Good luck with that. Are you planning to dispose of Burger Jackson and his friends?'

'I hope I can show them that not all magical creatures are evil and some can be our friends.'

Sir Philip decided to enter the conversation. 'In Concordia we're training wyverns to carry our knights. Now we've developed the new, lighter, armour, we think they could make an extraordinarily strong force.'

Burger Rowles looked startled. 'I hope this does not mean you're planning to invade Harbourtown.'

Sir Philip smiled. 'No, we have problems with wild tribes to the north of Concordia. We hope to convince them to remain peaceful. Harbourtown should profit from extra trade between Falconia and Concordia. You should build a road through the forest; it would save weeks of travel around it.'

Burger Rowles gave a grim smile. 'We've tried that several times over the years with the same result each time. The survivors gave up.'

'Survivors?' Sir Philip asked.

'And there weren't too many. What with shadow walkers, goblins, werewolves, and who knows what else that kept attacking the builders. We decided it wasn't worth it.'

Colin joined the conversation. 'I could use some of the crystals to protect the builders.'

Burger Rowles chuckled. 'I can just see that happening in the near future.'

'Strange events are happening,' Colin told him. 'Who knows how they'll affect the future.'

'Hmmm,' Burger Rowles replied. 'Anyway, we should all go to sleep. We have another long day tomorrow.' He called out to the constables, 'Morris, organise a night watch between the four of you.'

Morris called back, 'Do we have to, sir? Won't this magic screen thing protect us?'

Colin answered, 'It won't stop hostile beings, just slow them down so we can more easily take care of them. We still need a watch.'

Morris got up and spoke to the other constables. 'Alright, you men, Get some sleep. I'll take first watch.' Everyone except Morris bedded down for the night.

It was the second watch when they came. Jenny sensed them first. She gave a whinny which roused the dozing constable who was on watch. He opened his eyes to see a very slow-moving arm and leg dressed in black entering the yellow screen. He drew his sword, while shouting, 'To arms, we are being attacked.' The others woke immediately grabbing their weapons and looking for the danger. Charlotte went to Sir Philip, preventing him from standing, and stood over him with a long knife. The constable who had been on watch had meanwhile stabbed the slow-moving, black-clad torso of the man who had been entering the screen. He very slowly crumpled to the ground. Three other sets of black-clad limbs had now started to enter the camp. Each set ended up like the first as the men from Harbourtown took their toll. No more entered. A spear tried to enter and the companions watched in fascination as it slowly tipped down to fall just inside the boundary. There were no more incursions. Charlotte asked Burger Rowles, 'Who were they?'

The burger answered, 'Shadow walkers. Now they know we're waiting for them, they probably won't attack again, but we can't be too careful.'

After waiting for half an hour, Burger Rowles doubled the guard with both himself and Colin taking a turn. No one really slept well, but there was no more trouble that night.

CHAPTER 23

The next morning the group prepared a hot breakfast. There was little conversation, but no-one could not avoid the occasional glimpse of what seemed like partial bodies on the edge of the yellow screen of the dome. They broke camp and all except Colin saddled and mounted their horses. They all drew their swords, even Sir Philip, so as to be prepared for whatever may be outside the yellow dome. Colin then removed the large crystal from the staff. The screen disappeared immediately. There was a stampede of small creatures, that looked a lot like rats, into the forest. They had been feasting on the parts of the bodies that had been outside the dome. It was a grisly sight and Charlotte had to close her eyes. There was no sign of anything or anyone else in the area. Colin quickly gathered up the smaller yellow crystals from around the boundary and placed them back in his bag. He then took the staff and mounted his horse. They left the clearing following the path to the west.

The path varied in width throughout the day from only just being wide enough for a single rider to wide enough for two to ride abreast. One of the constables rode point and another rear-guard.

During one of the wider sections of the path, Colin was riding next to Charlotte. 'Colin, why didn't any of the silver creatures help us when we were attacked last night?'

Colin was quiet for several seconds in thought. 'The screen slows everything down, including magic. The fight was over before any of the silver creatures could appear and, even if they had, when they exited the screen, they would also have been moving very slowly making themselves an easy target. They can be killed.'

Charlotte gave a small start of surprise. 'I would hate that, I just hope they are careful.'

Colin answered, 'They were created to protect you. They would all get themselves destroyed to make sure you live.'

Charlotte rode on thoughtfully.

During another wide section of the path Burger Rowles

rode next to Sir Philip who was now feeling stronger. 'She likes you, you know.'

Sir Philip blushed. 'I like her too. I just want to keep her alive.'

Burger Rowles nodded. 'Don't we all. Do you think we'll achieve that by going to Falconia?'

'I hope so,' Sir Philip answered. 'Charlotte told me that the harpies that grabbed her told her that they wanted to kill her for Princess Scarlett; so did the wraith, but neither mentioned Queen Katerina. I just hope that Princess Scarlett is acting without her mother's knowledge and the queen will stop all this trouble.'

'Hmmm.' Burger Rowles rubbed his chin. 'Well, I must say from what I've heard about Queen Katerina, that if she was trying to kill Charlotte, she would be dead already. Queen Katerina has the reputation of not making mistakes.'

'My thoughts also,' Sir Philip disclosed. 'From the little I've seen of Princess Scarlett, she seems like a spoiled brat whose impetuous nature leads her to make mistakes. I just hope she keeps making them.'

'Me too, as it gives us a chance.' Burger Rowles paused. 'Why did King Regis pick you for this mission?'

'Would you believe for my charm and negotiating skills?' Sir Philip laughed. 'Actually, I'm just supposed to break the ice. The real negotiators will or would have followed. The way things are going that may never happen.'

'Yes, but why you specifically?'

'Well, it's a long and dangerous journey from Concordia to Falconia and I'm one of the best knights in Concordia.' He shrugged. 'I also have Jenny.' He rubbed Jenny's ears which twitched in response. 'Jenny isn't magical but is probably the cleverest and bravest horse on the continent.' Jenny gave a little skip as if in acknowledgement. 'Being King Regis' nephew helps give me some authority to speak for him and, finally' — Sir Philip paused — 'it was known in Concordia that Queen Katerina had a daughter and I, being an extremely eligible bachelor ... well, I was supposed to use my charm to help get the trade agreement, for starters.'

Burger Rowles gave Sir Philip a sharp look. 'You mean you were to court Princess Scarlett?'

Sir Philip grimaced. 'I think that was the idea, but I met Charlotte and that part of the king's plan I had decided to abandon, even before I met her sister.'

'Are they that much alike?' Burger Rowles asked.

'Yes,' Sir Philip answered, 'but only in looks. Their characters are hugely different. Charlotte leaves Princess Scarlett for dead.'

'I just hope we can leave Princess Scarlett for dead for real. It will solve a lot of problems.'

'Yes, it would.' The path narrowed again.

They were fortunate late that afternoon to find a small clearing for their camp site that night. Colin set up the yellow screen again, after they had collected enough firewood to last the night. Two of the group were on watch together all through the night, with even Sir Philip taking a turn in what was, fortunately for them, an uneventful night.

Back at the old and gnarled tree where the wraith had met Lickspit and Flatnose, redcap goblins were assembling. There were thirty-seven of them, all wearing red overalls, caps and red boots. Their leader was an old, but very strong, goblin. He was also very tall for a redcap goblin, three feet and seven inches. His name was Loftynut. He was talking animatedly to the wraith. 'We will always obey the great queen if we can, that is obvious, but what do we get out of it?' He spread his arms.

The wraith replied, 'As I said before, human flesh tastes good, as does horse. You will have a great feast and, what's more, don't forget this will mean that the queen will owe you a great favour. This could be a great asset for you in the future.'

'Ha,' Loftynut answered with a laugh. 'The queen is not famous for repaying favours.'

The wraith nodded. 'True, but she is famous for terrible punishments for those who defy her will. What would you prefer, a possible great favour or a certain terrible punishment?' The wraith smiled.

'Oh, well, if you put it like that,' Loftynut replied, thoughtfully. 'The feast sounds good at least. What do you want us to do?'

'We need a good place for an ambush. There are eight of them.' The wraith had scouted out the humans' position earlier that day. 'But the girl has help. She can call upon a pair of dolphins.' The redcap goblins all laughed at this as a pair of dolphins would be no good in the forest. 'And an eagle. It's not an ordinary eagle. This eagle is a giant eagle' — the wraith spread its claws — 'and very strong. We need to attack them in a heavily forested place where the eagle cannot help them.' The wraith did not know about Bruno the bear, or Jason the wolf. Before the wraith could continue, a redcap ran from the forest into the meeting and pointed back where he had come from. Breathless, he spluttered, 'They are camped three miles east of the ford on the River Thracks.'

Loftynut rubbed his hands together. 'That's good, after they cross the ford a couple of miles on this side of the river, the track leads through very heavy forest for at least half a day. No large bird would be able to get through that forest canopy. There are dozens of good places for an ambush.'

'That sounds perfect. There are eight of them and thirty-eight of you; thirty-nine of us when you include me. That's almost five to one, and we'll have the advantage of terrain and ambush. I hope you will all enjoy your feast tomorrow. Now, let us prepare.' He left with the goblins cheering.

In Falconia, the queen had summoned Princess Scarlett. Princess Scarlett had spent the last two days getting angrier and angrier, between searching her rooms with her servants for her half of the pendant, and the queen's library hoping to find an easy way to kill her sister. She was in the library when she was summoned. The queen was in the Throne Room sitting on her Throne. She had ordered all her courtiers and guards to leave so that they would be alone. The queen stretched out her hand, palm up. 'Well, the Great Ring of Falconia, I would like it back.'

Princess Scarlett blanched. 'It is still being used, mother.'

The queen suppressed her anger. 'For how long?'

'I hope to have it for you tomorrow.'

'Hope to have it tomorrow! What do you mean "hope"? What do you mean "tomorrow"?' the queen shouted, then held her hands, palms out in front of her. 'No, don't tell me. I must not know. Just bring me good news tomorrow.' The queen sighed. 'Now, get out.'

Princess Scarlett left, angry herself. She headed back to the library. She needed more knowledge.

CHAPTER 24

Early the next morning, Burger Rowles and the rest of the group had breakfast and broke camp. Colin took down the yellow screen and packed the crystals away. Once again, he kept the staff. They all mounted and set off to continue their journey to Castle Falconia. After about half an hour, they crossed the ford on the River Thracks. It was a shallow ford and the river flowed slowly. It was about ten yards wide. Sir Philip thought how different the river looked at this point from the rapids he had crossed just over a week ago. After crossing the ford, the forest got denser and darker. The track still led west, but was becoming narrower. Even though occasionally it was still possible for two to ride abreast, it was much easier to ride in single file. One of the constables led, followed by Burger Rowles, Colin, Charlotte, Sir Philip, and the three other constables brought up the rear. They had re-entered the forest for about three quarters of a mile after the river crossing when suddenly the leading constable's horse reared up. The constable shouted, 'Wolf!' and drew his sword. Burger Rowles also drew his sword and moved up to join the constable, shouting, 'I'm coming, I'll help you kill it.' Colin, behind the two of them, started screaming, 'STOP! STOP, STOP,' and tried to move his horse to the front of the column. It was not possible, so he dismounted and moved between the two riders who were waiting, swords in hand, for the wolf to attack. Colin grabbed both of the horses' bridles. 'Stop, Stop. He's a friend.'

Burger Rowles and the constable had not moved towards the wolf. They were sitting on their horses with their swords drawn just watching it. It was twice the size of an ordinary wolf and jet black. It was on its haunches looking as if ready to spring any second. Colin moved out from between Burger Rowles and the constable. 'Jason, how are you.' He moved forward and tickled the wolf under its chin and then rubbed its ears. The wolf gave a series of quiet barks and growls to which Colin listened very carefully. Colin then turned and walked back to the riders who had now bunched up as well as they could on the narrow trail.

Burger Rowles shook his head. 'This will be another charge against you when we get back. Consorting with monsters is a serious crime in Harbourtown.'

Colin replied, 'As I said before, it's just as well that we are in Falconia, and this monster' — he gestured towards Jason — 'has just saved all our lives. He brings a warning of an ambush by as many as forty redcap goblins in just over five miles down this path.'

'We must turn back,' Burger Rowles ordered. 'We should be able to outrun them.'

'They will know all the shortcuts,' Colin exclaimed. 'They live in this forest; they will catch us.'

'They might not bother. We'll have a head start. It would be too much trouble for them, and as leader of this group, I have made my decision,' the burger stated.

'Wherever Princess Charlotte is, that's where they'll attack. Don't you understand?' Colin glared at Burger Rowles. 'Princess Scarlett of Falconia wants her dead. All you have to do to save yourselves is give them Charlotte. Do you want to do that?'

Burger Rowles, recalling what he had been told by them two nights before, answered, 'Yes, you are right. What do you suggest?'

Morris, the constable who had been riding point, interrupted, 'Couldn't we just set up the yellow screen and wait them out?'

Colin shook his head. 'The crystals will only work for twenty-four hours at a stretch and, even if they did work longer, all the goblins would have to do is surround us until we starved.'

Sir Philip, who had moved up close to them, interrupted, 'I think we should give her to them.'

Burger Rowles angrily turned on him. 'You'll have to fight me first.'

Sir Philip smiled. 'No need for that, I may have a plan.' He turned to Colin. 'Can you ask Jason if he knows the positions of the goblins? We may yet surprise them.'

Colin went to talk to Jason. Bruno suddenly appeared and joined the wolf. 'I told you I saw a bear,' Morris murmured.

Sometime later, Burger Rowles was riding through the forest with two of his constables with Charlotte between the two constables. They were riding in single file even though the path at this point was almost wide enough for three riders abreast. Burger Rowles was shouting as he rode, 'We bring you Charlotte. Don't harm us,' repeatedly. He stopped a short distance of about twenty yards from where he had been told the ambush would take place. He repeated, 'We bring you Charlotte. Don't harm us,' twice more.

There was a rustling in the forest and eight redcap goblins came out onto the path. They crowded together. They were led by a goblin at least six inches taller than his companions. The tall goblin took two steps forward and addressed Burger Rowles. 'Tie her to a tree and ride away. We will not harm you.'

Burger Rowles looked down at him and asked, 'What guarantees do we have that you won't harm us after we give you Charlotte?'

The tall goblin stretched himself as tall as he could. 'I'll guarantee that you all will die if you do not obey me. However, you have the word of Loftynut of the redcap goblins that you may live if you obey.'

Just as Loftynut had finished making his declaration, the wraith slid out of the forest between the two groups, hissing, 'Where is Sir Philip and the others? He would not leave Charlotte for us. Where are they?'

Just as it had finished hissing, a boulder crashed through the trees from above. It hit three of the redcap goblins on their heads and shoulders who then fell to the ground, crushed. There was a loud screech as Great Wing flew off to find another boulder. The wraith hissed, 'We are tricked.' He pointed at Charlotte and ordered the goblins, 'Kill her!' Suddenly, there were loud noises and shouts from behind them. They stopped and turned.

As soon as Great Wing dropped the boulder, Colin, Bruno and one of the constables attacked the redcap goblins waiting in ambush on the left-hand side of the path from the rear. Colin was only armed with his staff, but Bruno made up for that by throwing goblins in all directions where they hit trees and landed in various unnatural positions. The constable with them also killed two before they realised what was happening.

On the other side of the path, Sir Philip, wearing just his breast and back plates for mobility, Jason and the other constable were attacking the other goblin ambushers from the rear. Jason was snapping at the goblins, crushing goblin skulls between his jaws, while Sir Philip seemed to think he was a berserker, swinging his battle axe around his head chopping bits off and killing goblins all around him, while screaming loud battle cries. The constable on this side was also making a good show of himself against the goblins.

The human and animal attackers started to force the goblins back towards Burger Rowles and his men. Loftynut and the five surviving redcap goblins ignored the wraith and went to help their comrades. Suddenly, Colin was cut down from behind and was stabbed half a dozen times. Bruno went crazy trying to get to Colin and killed at least half a dozen other goblins before he too was bought down, and Bruno died next to the prostrate body of Colin. The pendant around Charlotte's neck suddenly glowed and then formed a misshapen lump of silver. The constable who was with Colin and Bruno, although he fought bravely, was overwhelmed and also cut down and killed.

Sir Philip, Jason and the other constable who had headed back to join Burger Rowles and the others, encountered Loftynut and the other five redcap goblins that were with him. Jason bit the head off one while Sir Philip swung his axe down and cut a goblin almost in half from the shoulder to the hip. Loftynut leapt forward and stabbed the constable in the knee and the constable screamed as he fell to the ground. The goblins faced with a massive wolf with large teeth and a berserker with a battle axe, turned and ran to their companions in the forest. Sir Philip shouldered his battle axe and lifted the constable, who was still holding his sword, from the ground and carried him towards where he thought Burger Rowles had to be. Jason watched and covered their rear to make sure they made it.

Loftynut was regrouping the remainder of his goblins to make another attack when another boulder dropped through the trees hitting two more goblins and crushing them instantly. Great Wing might not have been able to fly down through the trees, but that did not mean he was out of the battle.

Burger Rowles, Charlotte and the two constables had dismounted and faced the wraith. The wraith, knowing that Sir Philip knew how to kill it, assumed he had passed this information to his companions and so was hesitant in approaching them. Looking at the looks of terror on the faces of the constables, it decided that it should be able to defeat them. It hissed at the group, 'Don't be stupid. Your friends cannot possibly beat forty redcap goblins. Be sensible, give her to me and ride away.'

Burger Rowles snapped at the wraith, 'We would rather die first. Charlotte, back to the trees with the horses, Bill to the left, Jack to the right. I'll be in the middle, and don't forget, go for the eyes.'

The humans all obeyed the burger's orders. Charlotte grabbed the horses the four had been riding and retreated to the trees, Jenny was looking after the other horses further back down the track, while Bill advanced on the left of the burger and Jack advanced on his right.

The wraith floated towards them. 'Fool, I will make you watch your men and Charlotte die and then I'll kill you very slowly.' Its claw suddenly flashed out and there was a beating piece of flesh in its claw. Jack looked down at the hole in his chest and slowly crumpled to the ground. The wraith smiled as both the burger and the constable stabbed at it with their swords, both missing its eyes. Its other claw flashed out and collected a twin to the heart in its first claw. Bill gave an appealing look at the burger as he too crumbled to the ground. The burger backed away towards Charlotte and the horses. He held his sword between himself and the wraith.

'Stop!' Sir Philip, Jason and the other constable came out of the trees. Sir Philip put the constable down. The constable lent against a tree. Sir Philip called to the wraith, 'It's you and me, wraith. You can kill them if you can kill me first.'

The wraith turned to face them. It looked at Jason. 'Another wolf. You get help from the oddest places.'

Sir Philip propped his battle axe against a tree and took the wounded constable's sword. He twirled it in his hand. 'Not as good as mine, but it'll do.'

Jason and the constable, who was limping, went to join Burger Rowles, as Sir Philip and the wraith faced each other. Loftynut and what was left of his redcap goblins, fourteen including himself, took that moment to come out of the forest.

'It seems we are destined never to fight,' the wraith hissed. It turned to the redcap goblins and pointed at Sir Philip. 'Kill him.'

The goblins started towards Sir Philip. The wraith moved towards Charlotte. Burger Rowles and the wounded constable, who had picked up one of the dead constable's swords, stood between it and Charlotte, swords in their hands. Another boulder fell through the trees killing two more goblins. Jason stood before Charlotte; his hackles raised. The burger and the last constable stood on either side of him.

There was a loud howl from the forest and five large wolves bounded out of it attacking the goblins, leaping at them and tearing out goblin throats left and right and even biting off heads. The goblins forgot Sir Philip as they were too busy defending themselves from the wolves. Sir Philip, knowing the wolves could take care of themselves, left them and ran at the wraith shouting a new war cry, 'For Charlotte!' The wraith stopped and turned just as Sir Philip's sword point entered it right between the eyes. The wraith gave out a great hiss and its smoky body slowly dissipated. A ring clattered to the ground which Sir Philip picked up. It showed the crown symbol of Falconia. He walked over to where Charlotte was standing, looking ashen, with the horses. He handed the ring to Charlotte who stood looking at it. Sir Philip told her, 'Put it on.' She did, placing it on the ring finger of her right hand. A burst of yellow radiance emitted from the ring as the band magically shrank to fit her finger. Jason, meanwhile, had bound across to help the other wolves dispose of what was left of the redcap goblins. Soon all the goblins and one of the wolves (not Jason) were lying dead. They had survived.

CHAPTER 25

At the very moment Charlotte put the Great Ring of Falconia on her finger, the queen was holding court in Falconia Castle. All the principal citizens of Falconia in all their best finery were there. The queen was in her role as the Chief Judge of Falconia. The full court was there because there was to be a grand banquet when she had finished. She was about to decide over a dispute concerning the ownership of a parcel of land outside the castle. She had already accepted the bribe that would influence her decision.

Just before she announced the decision, there was a sound like a thunderclap and the Throne Room darkened. A black whirlwind started to grow in the centre of the Throne Room. Everyone backed away from it. Most then turned and fled the room. In the centre of the whirlwind, a large, dark figure started to appear. Everyone left in the room were frozen to the spot with terror. The dark figure slowly continued to form from the top of the head down. The apparition became Braidos, the God of Chaos. His lower portion was not seen; the whirlwind still swirled below his waist. Some of the remaining courtiers fainted, others pointed and whispered his name, most just watched. He lifted his long, thin arm and pointed a long, slim finger at the queen. His voice when he spoke was loud and hollow. 'Your daughter has the Great Ring of Falconia.'

The queen gave a sigh of relief thinking that Princess Scarlett must have got it back. 'I know, I lent it to her.'

Braidos' laughter echoed throughout the room, his open mouth showing pointed teeth. 'Wrong daughter. You have broken our agreement. You have acted to harm her. You must be punished.'

The queen blanched and fell to her knees, her arms spread out, pleading, 'Give me time, I will correct this.'

'Too late, the damage is done.' The demon smiled as white lightning seemed to erupt from his finger and hit the queen. Huge flames suddenly sprang up around the queen and she screamed in terror and pain. To her remaining courtiers, petitioners and guards it looked like she shrank as the flames consumed her. Shortly, the flames disappeared and all that was left of the queen was a pile of ashes. Braidos looked around the room and then smiled as he shrank back into the whirlwind. There was another thunderclap as the whirlwind disappeared, and as the darkened Throne Room lightened there was no sign that it had ever been there except for the pile of ashes in front of the throne. Almost everyone who was left fled from the Throne Room.

The Royal Chamberlain, Sir John Amberleigh, was one of the few that did not run. He grabbed a page who had been shaking too much to run and ordered, 'Quick, go and get Princess Scarlett. She must be informed immediately. We must prepare a coronation and a funeral.' The page nodded and ran from the room.

Back in the forest, the human survivors of the battle were feeling amazed that they all were still alive. Sir Philip walked over to Helmut who, like the other werewolves, had resumed human form. 'That's three times you have saved me. I'll never be able to repay you.'

Helmut gave Sir Philip a smile. 'When Princess Charlotte defeats the queen and her sister, you can repay us by helping us live and trade with you humans and stop them hunting us.'

Sir Philip put his hand on his heart. 'You have my word.' He then shook Helmut's hand. 'But why are you here? We're miles away from your normal territory.'

Helmut smiled and nodded towards Jason. 'Our cousin called to us last night. We came immediately, it seems we got here just in time. It is also good that most of the redcap goblins have been destroyed. We were bitter enemies. Now we can be at peace with them.'

Burger Rowles who had been listening went to join them, He was embarrassed to be addressing two naked men and two naked females. He addressed all four, 'We have always been brought up to consider all non-human beings or monstrous animals as evil. I have seen this is not true. There are good and evil, just like us humans.' He put his hand on his heart. 'I hereby swear to you that I will do my best to change the laws of Harbourtown in order that you may visit and act like a free man.' Burger Rowles paused. 'I mean a free errr ...'

Helmut laughed and nodded his acceptance. 'You mean werewolf?'

Burger Rowles blushed. 'Er ... yes.'

Charlotte had gone back to her horse to get her medical kit. She bound up the surviving constable's knee after spreading a salve over it. Burger Rowles and the werewolves then all went looking for their dead in order to carry them to a place of burial or, in the case of the dead werewolf, a cremation pyre. Any wounded goblins they found were quickly dispatched to their ancestors. Sir Philip meanwhile walked back down the trail to where they had left the other five horses. He knew that they would be alright as he trusted Jenny implicitly to look after the other horses. Sir Philip was just returning with the horses when Burger Rowles suddenly shouted, 'I've found Colin. He's still alive.'

Everyone ran into the forest towards Burger Rowles' shout. Colin was lying there covered in blood. Sir Philip still had the green crystals tied to his arm and leg. He cut the crystals free and put them on the worst of Colin's wounds which were the ones in his chest and stomach. He also had wounds to the back and both arms and legs. Charlotte had meantime knelt next to Colin and placed a hand on both his chest and stomach. She had her eyes closed in intense concentration. Burger Rowles placed his hand on Charlotte's shoulder. She looked at him and he shook his head. Charlotte burst out in tears, 'Not true. Colin is strong, he will survive.' She went back to her concentration.

Sir Philip stated, 'There is always hope. I recovered

extremely fast using those crystals.'

Colin opened his eyes and looked at Charlotte. He croaked quietly, 'Charlotte, I must talk to you.' Charlotte leaned closer. 'Bring me my crystals.'

Charlotte turned. 'Colin needs his crystal sack.'

Burger Rowles turned and started running through the forest to the horses and was back within two minutes. Colin struggled to sit up supported by Charlotte and rummaged in the sack slowly with his wounded limbs. He took a purple crystal out of the sack. He grasped the half medallion that was hanging around Charlotte's neck. He placed the crystal on the medallion and mumbled a few words. The crystal glowed brightly for a second then went back to normal. Colin whispered to Charlotte, 'You must find the other half of the medallion and put the halves together. It will solve all your problems. This crystal will help.' Colin then placed his hands on the green crystals on his chest and stomach and mumbled more words. The green crystals started to glow. Colin smiled at Charlotte and then fell unconscious.

Helmut standing a little way apart spoke to the human survivors. 'You all must continue your journey. The sooner the queen and Princess Scarlett are defeated the better. We will do our best for Colin. I promise nothing.'

Charlotte covered all of Colin's wounds with salve

from her pack and then bound them up with bandages. She kissed Colin on the cheek, placed her hands on both his chest and stomach and whispered to herself, *If I have any magic, please work now for Colin. Make him survive.* She stayed like that for about fifteen minutes. She then got up and said, sadly, 'We must bury Bruno.' Everybody looked for the bear's body, even the werewolves, but it was never found. After half an hour of searching they gave up. 'No more of us must die,' Charlotte said, extremely firmly. 'Let's get this settled. We ride.'

Charlotte, Sir Philip, Burger Rowles, and Gerry the last surviving constable, set off again following the trail, leaving the dead goblins for the creatures of the forest. They all led one horse. On three were the bodies of the three dead constables and on the fourth they had supplies. The remaining horse was left for Colin if he recovered. The horse was not happy to be left with four werewolves.

Just before dusk fell, they finally came to the end of the trees. They all felt relieved to be able to set up camp not surrounded by the forest. They should hopefully reach Falconia Castle late the next day. They set a watch feeling slightly concerned that they were no longer protected by Colin's screen, then cooked dinner and went to sleep.

⚮

At the castle Princess Scarlett was in the Throne Room. She sat on her mother's throne, but she was in a state of shock. She had been told of the strange, tragic event that had cost the life of her mother and had ordered her ashes to be placed in a marble-lidded urn. Her mind was in a turmoil. Her twin sister had the Great Ring of Falconia. That surely must mean that the wraith's attack with the redcap goblins had failed and the wraith itself must be dead. What could she do to kill Charlotte? She thought about trying to make a bargain with Braidos who had killed her mother, but as yet she wasn't skilled or powerful enough. Besides, Braidos had just killed her mother and she would have to wait a while before contacting him. She knew her powers would increase in four days' time, her sixteenth birthday. She should be able to make a deal then. What was she to do until then, at least to slow her sister down? She suddenly thought of the locked door in her mother's, now her, laboratory. Her mother's monsters that she had created at least fourteen years before resided there. She would order them to stop Charlotte. She went to leave the Throne Room but was stopped by the Royal Chamberlain.

'Your Highness, I must talk to you.'

Princess Scarlett, who was in a hurry to get to the laboratory, snapped, 'Can't it wait?'

'I'm afraid not, Your Highness.'

'Oh, very well.' Princess Scarlett stepped back up onto the dais and again sat on her mother's throne.

The Royal Chamberlain ordered everyone else that was there out of the room. When they had left, he addressed Princess Scarlett. 'Your Highness, protocol demands that you do not sit on the Throne until you are crowned queen.'

'DEMANDS! DEMANDS! You dare to criticise me. Prepare to die!' Princess Scarlett stood and screamed.

The Royal Chamberlain flung himself onto his stomach and, in a trembling voice, cried, 'Please forgive me, Your Highness. I served your mother well as I would do the same for you.'

Princess Scarlett hesitated; she needed someone to run the day-to-day routine of the castle while she disposed of her sister. 'I will forgive you this once because of the service you did for my mother. I owe you no favours. Slip up once more and you will die horribly. Now, stand and tell me what you wanted.'

The Royal Chamberlain scrambled to his feet and bowed. 'Your coronation needs to be organised, Your Highness, and your mother's funeral.'

'Bury my mother tomorrow, next to my father. That should keep her happy; they can talk for eternity.' She gave herself a wicked grin thinking of how her mother had brutally sacrificed her father. 'The coronation can be in four days' time, on my sixteenth birthday.'

The Royal Chamberlain was aghast. 'Only four days! It cannot be done. And your mother, what ceremony should be done to honour her?'

Princess Scarlett shrugged. 'It does not matter. She's dead. Who cares? You have four days to prepare for my coronation. Make it good or else.'

The Royal Chamberlain very nervously said, having been present at the demise of the queen and knowing it was missing, 'We will need the Great Ring of Falconia for the coronation, Your Highness.'

Princess Scarlett gave him a withering glare. 'You will have it! Now leave me! Oh, and let it be known that I am to be called Your Majesty in future.'

The Royal Chamberlain bowed. 'Yes, Your Majesty.' He turned and headed for the door. Just before he got there, he turned back to the princess. 'Your Majesty, which god's representative do you wish to preside at the ceremony?'

Princess Scarlett thought to herself. If she chose Craidos, the God of Order, she would offend Braidos, the God of Chaos, and she would need him to help her in the future; but Braidos had just dramatically and very publicly killed her mother. It would not be very politic to choose him at the moment. There were more minor deities, but she didn't want any of those. 'You will preside at all official ceremonies until further notice,' she told Sir John. 'It will be a great honour for you. Do not fail in your duties.'

Sir John Amberleigh bowed. 'Thank you for this honour, Your Majesty.' He turned and rushed from the room. Princess Scarlett watched him leave and went to open a locked door.

CHAPTER 26

Princess Scarlett (she was not yet queen as much as she wanted to be) stood in front of the locked iron door in her laboratory. When she had entered the laboratory, she stopped and looked around. It was now hers. The library was now hers. No more having to clean up after herself. Servants could do that now. SHE was going to be queen! She had looked inside all the doors in the laboratory except this one and, to be honest with herself, she did not understand most of what she had seen inside the rooms, but now she stood outside the iron door and she did know what was behind this one.

She did not have the key but did not need it. She stared at the door for about five seconds and it flew open. Behind the door stairs led down into darkness. She picked up a candelabra of eight candles, clicked her fingers and all the candles lit. She started to climb down the stairs carefully as there was no banister. The stairs went down for about ten feet, then opened into a large chamber about twenty yards square.

There were tables, chairs and beds in the room, all extra-large and made of iron. Near the back of the chamber the shadows moved mysteriously. Shuffling noises came from the moving shadows. Princess Scarlett put the candelabra down on one of the tables and clapped her hands. A ball of light appeared in the centre of the room near the roof. The light from the ball reached every dark corner of the room. At the back of the room there were two strange skeletons on the floor and five of the strangest creatures Princess Scarlett had ever seen. All looked like someone had taken bits of animals and stuck them together without thinking.

One that had the head of a lion, the torso of a bull and the legs of an elephant, stepped forward and bowed to Princess Scarlett. 'You come with a message from the queen?'

'No, the queen is dead. I am her daughter, soon to be the new queen. Princess Scarlett.' Princess Scarlett pointed to herself.

The lion-headed creature answered, 'We knew you

were the queen's daughter as we recognised the scent of your blood. We are sorry the queen is dead. Even though she has kept us locked up here for years, she still provided for our needs. I am Sharag. This is Petra,' It gestured to a creature that had the head of a Great Dane, the body of a crab together with very nasty looking pincers, and massive chicken feet. 'This is Daisy.' It had the head of a cow, the body of a large, black bird with massive wings and the feet of a cat. 'She can actually fly, although she has not had the chance to do so for many years. This is Grunt.' It pointed to a creature with the head of an aardvark, the body of a chimpanzee and the legs of an antelope. 'And finally, this is Grant.' It patted Grant on the shoulder. Grant had the head of an ant, the body of a Siamese cat and the legs of a mouse. 'We sometimes have problems with Grunt and Grant as they do not like each other.' The creatures were not in normal proportions but were all about eight feet tall.

Two of us have died over the years.' It pointed to the two strange skeletons on the floor. 'There are, or were, four others of our kind that live, or lived, in the moat. What do you want of us?'

Princess Scarlett thought to herself for a few minutes. None of the creatures moved. She finally told them, 'I am going to free you so that you may roam the outside world and no longer be confined to this dark room.' The creatures all muttered gratefully. Princess Scarlett lifted her hands for silence. 'However, I have one task for you all first.' She waved her hands towards one of the walls. The wall began to glow and a picture formed. It was of Sir Philip when he was in the Throne Room. 'This man and his companions must die. There are several of them; one is a female of my age who, in fact, looks like me. I do not have an exact number of the group, but I am sure you all will be strong enough to kill everyone. I will supply you all with whatever weapons you wish. After you have killed them, I want you to bring back their bodies, their horses and every item they have bigger than a small pin, here to me. After you have completed this task, I will give you land where you may roam to your heart's content and have no problems from humans.'

The creatures all bowed to the princess. Sharag, the lion-headed one remained the spokesman. 'We thank you for your generosity, Princess. Where may we find these people?'

The princess thought, *They will be approaching from the north-west or west.* She said, 'I will send out scouts to look for their approach and let you know where they are.'

'Daisy can fly. She will also look and if she spots them, she will tell us where they are.' Daisy nodded.

'Good, come with me and I will equip you for your mission.' Princess Scarlett led the way out of the cellar. For the creatures it was the first time they had left the room for over fifteen years. They were all promising themselves that they were never going to return. Princess Scarlett was thinking that her sister, Sir Philip and whoever was with them would not stand a chance against these monsters. She thought about another card she had to play. Better to have more than one option. After she had supplied these foolish creatures, with whom she had no intention of living up to her end of the agreement, their equipment, she would go to her mother's, no, her library now, as was the laboratory, to find how to play it.

Charlotte woke up sweating. She stood up. She was back in the forest. Alone. Sir Philip, Burger Rowles, Gerry and the horses had all disappeared. She was in a small clearing surrounded by dense forest. Up above she could see a full moon which lit up the area. She whirled round as a hissing noise came from behind her. A wraith floated out from behind a tree. Charlotte screamed and backed away. The wraith moved towards her; its claws outstretched. She had seen what a wraith's claws could do and she was very afraid. There was another hissing sound from her left and then one more from her right. Two more wraiths had appeared.

She turned and ran into the forest. She was running for her life. The trees seemed to be against her, trying to bar her way. Branches came from nowhere, knocking her down and scratching her arms and face. Blood started to run down her arms. As fast as she ran, the hissing noise the wraiths made continued to follow her. She suddenly ran into a large, grassy clearing brightly lit by the moon. She stopped in the centre and hunched over, fighting to regain her breath. She looked up at the forest on the other side of the clearing. More wraiths had appeared from the other side. She was in the centre of the clearing while eight wraiths surrounded her at the forest's edge. They did not approach her, but seemed to hover, watching her. The moon seemed to get brighter. Charlotte looked up at it. She could not believe it.

The moon was growing. It got bigger and bigger as if getting closer, and as it got closer it started turning into a head. A face was forming. It was her, Charlotte. The face was her own. It loomed large above her, smiling. The mouth opened and laughter sounded in the clearing. Charlotte saw the teeth in the mouth. They had been sharpened. The opening behind them was a dark chasm.

The mouth moved towards her, threatening to envelope her. A giant, rough tongue flicked out from the mouth and licked the blood off her face and then she was half in the mouth. It closed as far as her stomach, the sharp teeth holding her in position. The teeth started to move horizontally, sawing into her stomach and back. Charlotte screamed and screamed and screamed as she was slowly sawn in half by the teeth.

'Wake up. Wake up.' She was on the ground being shaken very roughly by Sir Philip. 'Are you alright? What's happening? You were screaming.' Burger Rowles and Gerry were also standing about her looking exceptionally concerned.

'It was so real, I'm still alive.' Charlotte was shaking uncontrollably. There was blood on her arms and face. Her riding dress was torn around her stomach and back which were also covered with blood.

'It looks like whatever happened was real. You are really injured. What happened?' Sir Philip asked. Burger Rowles had got their medical supplies from the supply horse.

Charlotte still shaking, whispered, 'Not now. I can't talk about it. It was awful. It seemed so real.'

Sir Philip frowning, replied, 'Whatever it was that happened, it was real enough to harm you. Now sit. Gerry, get her some water.'

Sir Philip and Burger Rowles fixed up the wounds using lotions and liniments that Charlotte had brought from her apothecary. They also made her some herbal tea. 'These will fix her physical injuries, but whatever happened in her head ...' Burger Rowles shrugged his shoulders. 'One of us will have to watch her while she is asleep.'

Sir Philip nodded, 'Yes, we need to finish this Scarlett quickly.'

This Scarlett was at that very moment cursing and stamping her feet. *So close,* she thought, *so close.* Charlotte had almost been dead. A few more seconds and it would have been all over. It was a good spell she had discovered in the library. She would use it again in the future on other enemies. For now, it was a pity she had only the one lock of Charlotte's hair. One good thing, she now knew exactly where they were and how many. She would let her monsters know. They would all be dead yet and she would get her ring back. In just over three more days she would be queen.

CHAPTER 27

The next morning the small band had a quick breakfast, broke camp and continued their journey towards Falconia Castle. Everyone was extremely concerned for Charlotte and no one had gotten any sleep after Charlotte's very real nightmare. Charlotte was still badly shaken from the night's incident and because of her wounds, which now could be seen more plainly in daylight and were extremely painful, they took the journey slowly. They still travelled faster across the grassy hills than they had in the forest and every now and again they spotted a flock of sheep grazing.

After just less than two hours of travelling they came across a small walled town. The wall was made of stakes with about eight feet showing above the ground. It was made in much the same way as Sir Philip's palisade in the forest, but of much better quality and size. There was a double gate, which was large enough to allow a wide, bulky wagon through it. It was standing open with just two guards armed with pikes standing outside. The guards wore dark-blue uniforms and had front and rear body plates and open helmets. They were just lounging about chatting with each other and people seemed to be going in and out of the town without being challenged. However, they both quickly came to attention when they saw a group of strangers leading horses, on which there were three dead bodies. Sir Philip had taken the lead and led two of the horses with dead bodies, followed by Gerry with one horse with a dead body, then Charlotte, with Burger Rowles bringing up the rear with the pack horse. The two guards shouted into the village as they brought their pikes to bear at Sir Philip. Two more guards and a sergeant ran out of the gate from the town. The sergeant a very tall, about six feet five inches tall, slender, brown-haired man, approached Sir Philip. The sergeant asked in a loud, authoritarian voice, 'Who are you and what do you want?' But before Sir Philip could answer, he also asked, 'And what happened to those dead bodies?'

While this was happening, the others had ridden up to join Sir Philip. Suddenly the sergeant flung himself to his knees. 'I'm sorry, I'm very sorry, Your Highness. I did not recognise you at first. Please forgive me.' He waved for the guardsmen to lower their pikes and bow. He had seen Charlotte. 'We did not know you would be visiting us here. Were you ambushed?' he asked with concern, looking at the dead bodies and Charlotte's injuries. Sir Philip, taken completely by surprise at the turn of events, was still searching for something to say as the sergeant got up and continued, 'Quick, take those spare horses.' He shouted at his men, 'Help the princess, they have obviously been attacked. Andrew,' one of his men halted. 'Get the mayor and the healer immediately. Hurry.' Andrew immediately ran back inside the gate. He turned back to Charlotte. 'Please enter Thomastown, Your Highness.' He bowed and invited with his arms.

Charlotte smiled. 'Thank you,' which drew a look of surprise from the sergeant.

The other guards all dropped their pikes on the ground as they rushed to obey the commands. The sergeant led them inside the gate. Sir Philip saw as they were led in that all the buildings were made of wood. Wood obviously was plentiful, the forest being so close. Also, Sir Philip noticed that there were platforms inside next to the walls, so that defenders could look over the top of the wall for defence. The spare horses which carried the dead constables and the pack horse were taken from them. They continued along the road from the gate which led directly to the centre of the village. As they rode, the villagers started to line the street. None were cheering, but all bowed as they passed. In the centre of the village was a large two-storey, stone building from which an older man wearing a gold chain ran towards them. Sir Philip thought this must be the mayor. The mayor prostrated himself on the ground. He looked up. 'Please forgive us, Your Highness. We did not expect you. Especially with your coronation only three days away.'

Sir Philip by this time had composed himself. He dismounted and helped the mayor up. Sir Philip told the mayor, 'We wish to talk to you in private, immediately.'

The tall, white-haired mayor got up and answered, 'Certainly, at once. Please enter our modest town hall. The healer is on his way to tend to Princess Scarlett and refreshments will be served immediately.'

As the others dismounted, Sir Philip whispered to them that they should all say nothing until he thought it was safe. They followed the mayor inside the stone building and were led into a moderately sized, but lavishly furnished, hall. Murals of the forest and woodcutters covered all the walls and ceiling. There was a large table in the hall and well-padded, red-clothed chairs for twenty people. Servants were busily bringing in plates of cold food and large cups of various drinks. They were informed that warm food would be available shortly. The mayor went and sat on the largest of the chairs, which was at the head of the table. He looked at Charlotte and then jumped up in horror. 'I'm sorry, Your Highness, please forgive me. It was thoughtless of me.' He dusted his chair with his handkerchief and gestured for Charlotte to sit there, which she did. Sir Philip sat on her right and Burger Rowles on her left. Gerry sat a couple of seats further down and grabbed a leg of cold chicken off one of the plates. The mayor moved too and sat at the other end of the table from Charlotte. 'To what do we owe the honour of your visit, Your Highness, and what can we do to assist you?'

Sir Philip answered, 'Tell the servants to leave. What we have to say is a secret.'

The mayor stood, clapped his hands and shouted, 'Everybody out and lock the doors. Immediately, now, quickly.'

While the servants and guards were leaving, a stooped, old man with some wispy, white hair covering a mainly bald head and carrying a leather bag, entered. The mayor looked questioningly at Sir Philip. 'This is Healer Woodcraft. Would you like him to leave or stay?'

Sir Philip gave Healer Woodcraft an appraising look. 'Is he trustworthy?'

The mayor nodded. 'Completely! I have known him since I was a child.'

Sir Philip replied, 'He may stay and look after Charlotte.'

The mayor and Healer Woodcraft looked at each other in puzzlement. The mayor mouthed, 'Charlotte?' He looked at Sir Philip. 'Er ... don't you mean Princess Scarlett?'

Sir Philip had decided to lay the facts bare immediately. 'The princess you see before you is not Princess Scarlett, but Princess Charlotte.'

'Is this a joke? There is no such person as Princess Charlotte,' the mayor exclaimed, rising from his seat.

Sir Philip answered, 'She exists alright. There she is.' He pointed at Princess Charlotte. 'They are twins, and the queen and Princess Scarlett have been trying to kill Princess Charlotte without success.' He paused. 'What's this about a coronation?'

'The queen is dead. Princess Scarlett is to be crowned in three days' time on her sixteenth birthday,' the mayor stated. 'Everyone in Falconia knows this.'

Charlotte murmured, 'That's right, I am sixteen in three days.'

'I'm sure you are an imposter. I'm going to send a messenger to the princess,' the mayor declared, pointing at Charlotte.

Healer Woodcraft put his hand on the mayor's shoulder. 'Wait, Paul, the circumstances could be just what we have been waiting for.' He turned to Sir Philip. 'The queen was hated and feared. Princess Scarlett is hated, but not feared as much. This could be our chance to get rid of her. We could use your imposter to get close to the princess and kill her or at least start a rebellion. As I said, the people hate her as much as they did her mother.'

Sir Philip could feel himself getting angry. 'Princess Charlotte isn't an imposter. We will accept your help, however, to put Princess Charlotte on the throne.'

Charlotte, who was only just getting used to being called a princess, exclaimed, 'What? Me, the queen? No, I just want to live in peace and go back to my shop.'

The mayor declared, 'We will work out who should take the Throne after we have deposed Princess Scarlett. It certainly won't be an imposter. Sir George would never agree.'

At this point there was a loud knock on the door and they heard the door being unlocked. The sergeant with half a dozen guards burst into the room. The sergeant, breathless, addressed the mayor. 'Mayor Reading, there are five monsters outside the gate demanding that we send out these people, their horses, all their belongings and even the bodies of their dead. They say they represent Princess Scarlett.'

The mayor sighed and shrugged his shoulders. 'Well, it looks like nothing we spoke of before matters. We will have to give you to the monsters. If any of you repeat what we said, we will deny it and say you are trying to incriminate us because we wouldn't help you.'

Sir Philip started to draw his sword. Charlotte grabbed his arm and whispered to him, 'No, we will beat the monsters and we may need these people's help afterwards. Don't forget Jason and Great Wing.'

Sir Philip replied, 'You are right.' He smiled. 'When this is over you will make a great queen.' He glared at Mayor Reading. 'You will find out that she is not an imposter but the rightful queen.'

The sergeant raised his hand to his mouth and gave a small cough. 'Err ... Mayor Reading, we have a small problem. We have already buried the three Harbourtown constables.'

The mayor shouted at the sergeant, 'Well, dig them up. Quickly! Get them to the gate.'

The sergeant went to get the bodies while the mayor and the other guards escorted Charlotte, Sir Philip,

Burger Rowles and Gerry to the gate. Their horses and their belongings were already there. The mayor climbed a small ladder to the platform that overlooked the gate and shouted to the monsters that he was complying with their demands and the group would be forced to leave very shortly. A cart came down the street with the three dead constables still covered with the mud from their burial. They were unceremoniously thrown onto the backs of three of the horses. The gates were opened and the small group, at pike point, were forced to leave Thomastown to face the five monsters.

CHAPTER 28

The five strange creatures had been waiting patiently. All were heavily armed, three with swords and shields and two with axes and shields. They watched the group lead their horses through the gates and out of the town. The gates shut quickly behind them. The mayor and all able people manned the walls, not to defend them but to watch the fun. Sir Philip, who had been allowed to put on his full armour, mounted Jenny and ordered everyone, including Charlotte, to also mount. 'We'll have a better chance on horseback. It's a pity that Burger Rowles is the only one of us uninjured in any way.'

Gerry asked, nervously, 'Where are Jason and Great Wing?'

Charlotte replied, 'I'm sure they will be here when needed. Wait here, all of you.' Sir Philip started to protest, but she shook her head. 'I feel I must do this; wait.' She rode forward to meet the creatures leaving the others in front of the gate.

The creature with the lion's head strode forward to meet her. It was all Charlotte could do to hold her horse, Maria, steady. When they were three yards apart, the creature spoke. 'My name is Sharag. We have been sent here to kill you and take your bodies and belongings back to Falconia Castle for Princess Scarlett. Submit and we will make it as painless as possible.'

Charlotte looked down at Sharag and asked, 'Are you of the same ilk as Dobbin?'

Sharag roared, scaring both Charlotte and her horse which took a step back. Sir Philip and the others started to move forward, but Charlotte signalled them to stop.

Sharag stared at Charlotte. 'What do you know of Dobbin?'

'He was my friend for more than fifteen years. He more than once saved my life and I was with him when he was killed a week-and-a-half ago.'

'Dobbin is only just dead?' Sharag said, quietly shaking his head. 'We thought he had died years ago.' Sharag moved forward and examined Charlotte more closely.

'You look like the princess.' He sniffed. 'You smell of royal blood. How can this be?'

'I am the Princess Scarlett's twin sister, Charlotte, the rightful Queen of Falconia and I have the Great Ring of Falconia to prove it.' She raised her arm and twisted her hand showing both the creatures and the humans on the wall the Great Ring of Falconia. There was loud murmuring from the town walls.

The lion-headed creature bowed to her. 'Wait, my friends and I must talk.' He turned and went back to the four other creatures and they went into a huddle.

Sir Philip rode up to Charlotte and whispered, 'I thought you said you just wanted to go back to your shop.'

Charlotte smiled. 'It depends on the audience.'

The creatures broke up their huddle and Sharag came forward again. 'How did Dobbin die?'

Sir Philip answered, 'He died fighting alongside me, saving Princess Charlotte's life. He was a brave warrior.'

'That is true,' the lion-headed creature nodded. 'We cannot harm royal blood, but we cannot disobey the queen. Neither you nor your sister is queen at this moment in time. We have decided that we will not find you until after the coronation. Then we must follow the queen's commands, whoever the queen may be. Until then we will camp in the forest.' Sharag turned and joined the other creatures who then set off on a track leading east towards the Great Forest.

The gates to the village opened behind them. The mayor came out and walked towards Charlotte and bowed. 'I apologise once again, but this time not to Princess Scarlett, but to Princess Charlotte soon to be Queen Charlotte of Falconia.' He gestured towards the gate. 'Please come back in, we need to discuss the kingdom's future.'

Charlotte, Sir Philip, Burger Rowles and Gerry rode back through the gate leading the horses with the bodies and the pack horse with them. The mayor re-joined them inside the walls. 'Please come with me back to the town hall. Sergeant Clough, arrange to have these brave men reburied immediately.'

'Bury them, dig them up, bury them. I wish he'd make up his frickin' mind,' Sergeant Clough muttered.

Back in Falconia, Princess Scarlett was sitting on the queen's throne getting anxious. She and her servants had practically torn her rooms apart looking for her half of the medallion. Also, she still hadn't got the Great Ring of Falconia. Her monsters should fix that up for her. They must have killed, or shortly would kill, her sister and Sir

Philip and whoever else was with them. She should have the ring either today or tomorrow.

The Royal Chamberlain entered the Throne Room and bowed to Princess Scarlett. He, for some reason, decided to overlook the fact that she was sitting on the queen's throne rather than her own. 'Your mother's funeral will take place in an hour, Your Majesty.' Princess Scarlett waved a dismissive hand. 'Things are progressing well for your coronation. There is, however, one small problem.' The Princess glared at him. He swallowed. 'The Great Ring of Falconia should be displayed with the crown, the orb and the sceptre.'

'You will have it in the morning. Now, go!' she finished, with a shout. She thought to herself, *How many times is it now I have thought my sister is about to die and it did not happen. I must be prepared and take precautions.* She called for a page. 'Summon the Royal Jeweller. I want him here immediately. No excuses.'

In less than fifteen minutes the royal jeweller was there. He was a short, plump, pug-nosed man with long, red hair down past his collar. He had gold and silver rings on all his fingers, some with gems and some not. There were gold and silver earrings and studs in his ears and gold chains around his neck. He bowed low. 'How may I be of service, Your Highness?'

'You may call me Your Majesty. You know the Great Ring of Falconia?'

'Yes, Your High ...' He stopped himself just in time. 'Your Majesty.'

'I want a copy of it before breakfast tomorrow.'

The royal jeweller stammered, '... but, but, Your Majesty. It cannot be done.'

Princess Scarlett gave him a long, cold stare. 'You are not going to tell me that there is a problem, are you?'

'Of, of, course not, Your Majesty,' the jeweller stuttered.

'Good, you may go.' She waved a dismissive hand. 'I think you are going to be quite busy. I will see you first thing tomorrow.'

The jeweller bowed and left, a rather concerned look on his face. Princess Scarlett got up off her throne and went to her rooms. Her servants were in despair. They could not find the medallion. Princess Scarlett had three personal maids, all about her age. None of them were her friends. There were several girls whom she called friends, but they were really sycophants. She had no really true friends; in fact, she had not seen any of them since Sir Philip had kissed her in the market — she had been too busy. She entered her rooms. 'Well, where is it?' she demanded. There was no answer. She tightened her lips and pointed at one of her maids. The maid started to choke. Her hands went to her throat as she struggled to breathe. Then she fell to her knees as she started to turn blue. About thirty seconds later she was dead.

The Princess turned to the two others who were cringing in the corner of the room. Princess Scarlett scowled at the two girls. 'If the medallion is not found, one of you will die at this time tomorrow, the other at this time the day after. Get some guards to help you search, but find my medallion!' Princess Scarlett screamed. She turned to leave but stopped and looked at the body of her maid. 'Oh, and make sure you get this filth cleaned away before I get back.' She left.

Half an hour later, in the royal graveyard at the back of the castle where the kings and queens and the other royalty of Falconia had lain in magnificent tombs for over two hundred years, the queen's remains were buried next to the man she had secretly murdered. Sir John Amberleigh, the Royal Chamberlain, wearing black, presided. The pall bearers were half a dozen guards led by the Captain of the Guard, Gill Millard, and there were eleven of her courtiers present. The ceremony was the shortest funeral that had ever been performed in the

Royal Falconian Castle graveyard and without the pomp and ceremony that would have been expected for a royal burial, especially for a king or queen. Princess Scarlett was noticeable by her absence.

CHAPTER 29

Back at Thomastown, Sir Philip, Burger Rowles and Mayor Reading were in a huddle making plans in Mayor Reading's private rooms, while Healer Woodcraft tended to Charlotte and Gerry's wounds in the main hall, using his own and some of Charlotte's lotions from her bag which she had lent to the healer. When he had finished, Gerry limped off towards the kitchen. There was no one else in the hall, not even a guard. Healer Woodcraft said to Charlotte, 'I see that you get your herbal cures and teas from the Silver Apothecary in Harbourtown.'

Charlotte answered with a smile, 'Yes, I own it.'

Healer Woodcraft gave a start. 'What? You're Charlotte Silver? I met your mother, Julie, many years ago. I went to

Harbourtown because the Silver Apothecary had such a magnificent reputation and I was interested in what they had for sale. I have been importing your herbal medicines to supplement my own supplies for many years. I actually met you as a baby.'

Charlotte blushed and answered, 'Well, it's nice now we are on the same side, and I'm glad that you find our medical herbs so helpful. We go to a great deal of trouble to make sure we only sell the best. I'm a bit bigger now and circumstances have changed a great deal.'

'Yes, I heard that your parents were murdered. I'm very sorry,' Healer Woodcraft said quietly.

'It happened a long time ago,' Charlotte replied sadly.

Mayor Reading, Sir Philip and Burger Rowles re-entered the main hall and went to sit at the great table with Charlotte and Healer Woodcraft. Mayor Reading told them, 'The coronation is to be held in three days. All the towns, villages and mines have been ordered to send as many people as possible to Falconia Castle to celebrate the coronation. We will smuggle the four of you with our contingent into the castle. We will tell our contacts in other towns, villages and mines and, believe it or not, there are a lot of them, to be ready for an incident and to take advantage of it at the coronation without letting them know about you or exactly what it will be. Not that we really know ourselves.' He grimaced. 'We will spring you on everybody at the last minute to help make sure our plans do not get to Princess Scarlett's ears.'

Sir Philip asked, thoughtfully, 'Didn't the queen have a spy network that will now report to Princess Scarlett? They'd have at least one spy here in Thomastown.'

Mayor Reading smiled. 'Yes, that would be Leslie Thatcher. He makes a good spy; reports regularly without fail.'

Sir Philip and the other non-Falconians looked shocked. Healer Woodcraft smiled with the mayor. The mayor continued, 'He makes all of his reports to the Royal Falconer, Sir George Potts.' He smiled at Charlotte. 'Your great-uncle.'

'I have a great-uncle?' Charlotte asked, surprised.

The mayor answered, 'Well, Sir George, was er ... , is your father's uncle. I don't know about uncles on your mother's side of the family. Sir George was one of the greatest soldiers in Falconia. He saved your father's life at the Battle of Duchies Pass. That was about eighteen years ago.'

Charlotte asked, 'What happened?'

Mayor Reading sat in thought for a minute, then continued, 'It was the spring of the year four hundred and ninety-seven ...'

Sir Philip interrupted, 'Four hundred and ninety-seven? Do you have that right?'

'The Falconian calendar starts with the building of Falconia Castle.' The mayor shook his head. 'Everyone everywhere should use our calendar, then there wouldn't be any confusion.'

Sir Philip looked offended. 'And what is wrong with the Concordian calendar?'

'Well we're in Falconia, for one thing, and I'm talking to Princess Charlotte of Falconia, so we're using the Falconian calendar,' the mayor said, righteously.

Charlotte looked at Sir Philip and put a finger to her lips. Sir Philip crossed his arms with a grimace and remained quiet.

'As I was saying, it was the spring of the year four hundred and ninety-seven.' The mayor gave Sir Philip a withering look. 'Sir George was the commander of the King's Household Guard. I was one of his lieutenants. We received a pigeon at the castle telling us that the fortress at Duchies Pass was under siege from a force from the Duchies. They were mainly troops from Mayflor, but there were troops from the other Duchies as well. It took us completely by surprise as we'd been at peace for centuries.

'To be honest, Falconia wasn't ready for a major war.

All we'd ever fought since we beat the dwarfs over two hundred years before, were raiders from the Great Forest, mainly goblins of one colour or another. It took us two days to organise and collect men from nearby towns and villages and the mines. It took us another day of forced march to near the fortress.

'The fortress at Duchies Pass is built into the mountain itself, at the end of the pass. There are only walls on two sides and they are twenty feet thick and sixty feet high. The gate is made of thick oak and when closed there are massive blocks of rock that can be placed behind it to turn it into a solid wall. The gate is thirty feet above the pass floor and the only access is via a ramp which is only just wide enough for two wagons to pass abreast. The bottom thirty feet of the wall only protects the rubble that the inside of the fortress is built on, except for the tunnels and cellars at the back of the bastion. In other words, it's a hard place to take.

'King Edmond decided to rest our army next to Passville and march on the fortress the next morning. Pigeons had been exchanged between the fortress and Passville, so we knew it was still holding out. Before dawn the next day, we marched. As we neared the fortress, we heard explosions. Your grandmother was trying to blow holes in the wall.'

Charlotte gasped, 'My grandmother?'

Mayor Reading answered, 'Yes, the celebrated Duchess of Mayflor and, unfortunately, she still is, but to continue, the wooden gate had disappeared and only the stone blocks could be seen. Bits of the wall were everywhere and in some places the holes went all the way through. There was rubble, broken ladders and broken and dead men all along the wall. The duchies' troops were making an escalade assault on the wall.'

Charlotte interrupted, 'What's an escalade assault?'

The mayor answered, 'It's an assault using ladders for the troops to climb, so that they can get to the top of a wall, climb over it and hopefully kill enough of the defenders to establish a point where more troops can enter a defended fort or town and therefore take it, or at least force a gateway for more reinforcements. Your grandmother was using her powers to throw lightning to kill our men at the top of the wall to make it easier for her men to scale it. Our cavalry, which was mainly the Household Guard, charged the attacking soldiers while the king organised our infantry. As soon as the enemy troops saw us, they abandoned their assault and ran back to their lines in the pass. We pursued and cut down some of the stragglers, then a couple of explosive lightning blasts from the duchess blew several of us up and so we retreated to our lines.

The enemy formed a three-man deep shield wall to face ours and ...'

Charlotte interrupted again, 'A shield wall?'

Sir Philip answered her this time, 'It's when infantry form a line with interlocking shields to protect each other from an attacking force. The two walls clash and the first to break usually loses. It's strong against cavalry and the best way to win is to have a longer wall so you can overlap your opponents and start killing them from the flanks and behind.'

'That's right, but in a narrow pass there is no chance of an overlap.' The mayor continued, 'The duchess started to use her powers to blow holes in our shield wall. Fortunately for us, King Edmond had the Great Ring of Falconia on his finger. After the first lightning explosion, the ring intercepted all the duchess' attempts to damage our shield wall. It was amazing to watch. A bolt of lightning would flash towards us from the hands of the duchess and a ray of green light would emit from the ring and intercept it and an explosion would occur. The duchess soon realised she was wasting her time and energy and stopped, sending her infantry forward to meet ours. Neither side had much in the way of archers, although we probably had a few more than them. Why use archers when you've got someone who can blow holes in a shield wall. Our cavalry was arranged behind our shield wall so we could either counterattack any break in our wall or pursue if the other wall broke first. The duchies had hardly any cavalry behind their wall. We were very confident of winning.

Just as the shield walls were about to clash, out of what seemed nowhere the duchies' cavalry appeared behind us taking us completely by surprise. To this day I have no idea how their cavalry got behind us, but they did. They smashed into our cavalry and headed for the king. We lost many men in that first contact. Sir George, together with the King's Household Guard, which included myself, turned to keep the king safe. The king, who was still covering our troops with the Great Ring of Falconia, was about to get set upon by five of the enemy, when Sir George interceded between them and the king. He killed two of them almost immediately but lost his left hand in the process. He had taken on a third enemy, who slashed him across the face, which cost his left eye, when the king and several more of the bodyguard counterattacked and came to his assistance. It was at this time I was severely wounded in the stomach. I still suffer the effects of the wound, which is why I am so grateful for Healer Woodcraft's continued presence here in Thomastown.' He nodded towards the healer, who answered with a smile.

'The rest of the story was told to me later, after I had recovered. Our shield wall was being pushed back as our troop's confidence was waning because of the attack behind them. Our cavalry was holding up against theirs. Even though we were taken by surprise, we still had a very slight advantage in numbers. It was the pivotal point of the battle. Our men then sallied forth from the fort and attacked their shield wall from behind which caused it to break and then the duchies troops fled back to their camp losing many men in the process.' The mayor looked at Charlotte, who had put up her hand.

'I thought you said the fort's gate was blocked by stone blocks?' she asked.

Mayor Reading spread his hands next to his head and beamed, 'That was' — he paused — 'and is, an amazing feat of engineering. The stone blocks are put in place and removed by a series of rollers and pulleys along a ramp that ...'

Healer Woodcraft interrupted, 'Paul, I know you are excited by the engineering, but I'm sure our guests just want to get to the end of the story.'

Mayor Reading pulled a face. 'Alright, anyway their shield wall broke and they started to run back to their camp. Our troops followed, killing many in the process. Then it was our men's turn to die. The duchess had started to blow holes into our attacking forces who stopped the pursuit and retreated to our original lines. The garrison went back to the fort and waited. The enemy cavalry, realising they couldn't get back to their own lines, surrendered. Everything went quiet for about ten to fifteen minutes and then the duchess walked out by herself holding an olive branch. King Edmond, against all advice, dismounted and went out to meet her, also alone.

'They talked for over an hour. At the end, it had been agreed that we would forgive their transgression and return the prisoners we had. In return we received extra trading rights and King Edmond got to marry the duchess' daughter, Katerina. I think they got the best of the bargain.

'It took some time for Sir George to recover; when he did, he was appointed Royal Falconer ...'

This time it was Sir Philip who interrupted, 'Royal Falconer, isn't that a rather tame position for a man of Sir George's obvious capabilities?'

Mayor Reading smiled. 'It's the code for being in charge of the Falconian Intelligence Service. Myself, I was appointed a Deputy Mayor of Thomastown and I have worked myself up to be the mayor. We have all had cause to regret the agreement King Edmond made that day and now, hopefully, thanks to you' — he looked at Charlotte — 'we may be able to rectify the situation.'

Charlotte sat silently for a while and then lifted her medallion from around her neck and said, 'Colin said that we must find the other half of this medallion and we will win. Hopefully, that will not be too hard.'

The mayor took the medallion and studied it. He said, 'I can't believe it will be that simple.'

'Hope for the best. Prepare for the worst,' Sir Philip said. 'It will usually be something in between.'

The mayor stood and went to the door. He called for a servant, 'Bring wine, we are going to toast for a victory.'

Charlotte said, 'Water for me, please.'

When the drinks came, they all drank to victory.

CHAPTER 30

The next day, Thomastown was a hive of activity. Messengers were sent out to most of the towns and villages in Falconia. Disguises for Charlotte and Sir Philip were made. No one at the castle would know Burger Rowles or Gerry. It was decided to enter the castle the next day and stay at friends of Mayor Reading until the morning of the coronation and sneak into the castle along with the crowds. Mayor Reading and Healer Woodcraft would not be with them as they were VIP guests and their presence would be required in the Throne Room. After they had sneaked into the castle, they would use Colin's purple crystal to find the other half of the medallion as they hoped finding it and joining the medallion together would solve all their problems. If it didn't, Princess Scarlett being the popular person she was, they hoped the mayor and his friends could stir up the populace to rebellion against her, claiming Charlotte as the rightful heir as she had the Great Ring of Falconia. Charlotte didn't like either plan, but agreed it was all that they could do.

At the castle, things were even more hectic. VIPs and others were arriving from all over the kingdom. All the inns were full, and the less important invitees were camping in tents in the market square or outside the town walls. The castle kitchens were busy preparing food as were all the bakeries and eating places in the town grounds. Around the outside of the market square, the local farmers were doing a brisk trade selling fruit and vegetables. All the local businesses and especially the farmers and florists around Falconia were making a fortune.

Inside the Throne Room, Princess Scarlett watched as the coronation decorations were being set up. New tapestries were covering the walls, new rugs were being laid down and flowers were just about everywhere. Blue and green banners, the colours of Falconia, with the symbol of a falcon holding the Great Ring in its claws hung from the ceiling. The crown, mace, sceptre and Great Ring of Falconia were on a large, low, black-marble pedestal at the front of the throne dais. They rested on purple velvet pads. The Royal Jeweller had stayed up all night working on the ring, comparing his work with drawings and paintings of the ring, and had presented Princess Scarlett the ring before her breakfast. Fortunately for him, Princess Scarlett had a reputation for sleeping in and this gave him some extra time. If the ring was closely scrutinised, the differences could be seen, but Princess Scarlett was confident that wouldn't happen as no one was allowed on the dais without her express permission. She also expected that the real Great Ring of Falconia would be returned to her that day by Sharag and its companions.

Just after lunch she was getting enormously impatient when it still hadn't arrived. She sent for the Captain of the Guards. She met him in her private rooms behind the Throne Room as she did not want to interrupt the preparations. The captain entered her rooms and bowed. 'At your service, Your Majesty.'

'Captain Miland, I want you to send some scouts to the Thomastown area to find out what happened to the creatures I sent there to kill some of our kingdom's enemies.'

The captain bowed again. 'Certainly, Your Majesty. I will do so immediately. They should reach the area sometime tomorrow morning.'

'They will gallop all the way and reach the town tonight and be back here with a report tomorrow morning. Tell the mayor at Thomastown that I order them to provide the scouts with their fastest horses for their speedy return,' the princess said, with firm voice.

Captain Miland gulped. 'That is what I meant, Your Majesty. I will get them started at once.' He bowed and hurriedly left the room.

Princess Scarlett shook her head and thought to herself, *Why am I surrounded by incompetents?*

She returned to the Throne Room and sat on the Throne and watched the hustle and bustle of the preparations for her coronation. Sir John Amberleigh approached her and bowed. 'Everything is proceeding well, Your Majesty.'

Princess Scarlett nodded. 'So I see. I am pleased with you.'

'No expense has been spared. You will have the greatest coronation Falconia, no, the whole continent of Strasia, has ever seen.'

Princess Scarlett beamed down at him. 'You are doing very well indeed. Keep up this good work and I will be sure to reward you well.'

'And I see you have recovered the Great Ring of Falconia,' the Royal Chamberlain continued. 'May I step up and look at it?'

'No! You may not!' Princess Scarlett snapped, loudly enough so everyone stopped working to watch. 'Back to work, all of you!' she shouted. She looked back down at a now shaking and cowering Sir John Amberleigh and spoke quietly, but with menace. 'No one, I repeat no one, is to mount this dais until my coronation. Do you understand?'

'Yes, Your Majesty.'

'Good, now go back to work.'

Princess Scarlett turned and sat back down on the throne. Sir John Amberleigh went back to work, shaking.

Later, still angry, she went down to her rooms. All of them had just about been torn to pieces. Every piece of wooden furniture had been smashed. Every piece of fabric was torn open. The mattress stuffing was scattered all over her bedroom. The skirting boards had all been removed and there were holes in all the walls, floors and ceiling. Princess Scarlett had been sleeping in the best of the guest rooms. She looked at her maids. 'Well, where is it?'

The maids cowered in a corner, while the five guards

who had been helping them moved away. Princess Scarlett said, 'I assume this means you don't have it. Oh, well, Eeny, Meeny, Miny, Moe.' She played the game using her two maids. She pointed at one of the maids who fell to her knees sobbing and begging to be allowed to live. Princess Scarlett gave her a contemptuous look. 'Something different this time, I know.' She said out loud to herself, 'One from mummy.' She held her hands in front of her and closed them slowly. The maid's head imploded in a bloody ruin. Princess Scarlett gave the scene a disgusted look. 'I'd forgotten the mess. Oh, well.' She looked at the last surviving maid. 'Clear this up and then get back to the search. I will see you tomorrow.' She added as an afterthought, 'I will have to get the Royal Chamberlain to hire me some more maids. Don't stop working.' She left to go to her temporary rooms.

CHAPTER 31

'Sir, wake up, sir, it's urgent.' Sergeant Clough, in full uniform, was shaking Mayor Reading. They were in the mayor's bedroom on the first floor of the town hall. The sergeant had pushed aside the curtain on Mayor Reading's four poster bed.

The mayor rubbed his eyes and sat up. He was wearing a white nightshirt. 'What's the meaning of this?'

The sergeant answered, 'Sorry to disturb you, sir, but there's a pair of Falconian Castle messengers at the main gate with what they say is a message from Princess Scarlett.'

The mayor dragged himself out of bed. He was extremely worried but not panicked. 'Take them to the main council chamber. What's the time?' he asked, yawning.

'Just before midnight, sir,' the sergeant answered.

The mayor shook his head. 'You're not serious, surely. What do they want at this time of night?'

The sergeant ventured, 'Princess Charlotte, sir?'

'If they knew about Princess Charlotte being here, there would be an army out there, not two messengers.' The mayor rubbed his unshaven chin. 'Get Sir Philip. Oh, and make sure that neither of the messengers speak to anyone before I see them.'

The two messengers were both tall — one was dark and the other fair — and both wearing the Falconian livery of blue and green with the black falcon holding the Great Ring of Falconia in its claws, had been left waiting in the main Council Hall with Sergeant Clough. Mayor Reading met Sir Philip, who was not wearing armour but wore his sword, in a panelled anteroom of the Council Hall. The mayor said, 'Two messengers from Princess Scarlett are here. From here you can hear and see everything that is being said in the Council Hall.' The mayor slid one of the panels aside. 'Be prepared to grab Princess Charlotte and the others if necessary and be ready to run. Your horses are being made ready as we speak. I will try to hold them up while you escape.'

Mayor Reading entered the council chamber, threw his arms wide and, with a smile on his face, said, 'Sorry to have kept you waiting so long. What would Princess Scarlett want at this time of night from her loyal subjects of Thomastown?'

The fair-headed messenger answered, 'I am Sergeant Wilbur and this is Private Joseph. We have been sent to get information concerning enemies of the kingdom and about some strange creatures that were sent to apprehend these enemies. Do you have any knowledge of either group?'

Mayor Reading paused for several seconds. 'Five very strange creatures arrived here two days ago. They looked like someone had chopped up different animals and stuck them together again any old how. We didn't let them in, but I spoke to them from the top of the gate's rampart. The creature with a lion's head was their spokesman, er ... I mean spokes-creature. It said they were looking for some people — a man and a young woman and their companions. I told them that we hadn't seen them, and they then set off towards the forest, I assume in pursuit of them.'

The messengers gave a great sigh of relief. The sergeant said, 'You have some news. That's pleasing. We were afraid we would have to go back with no news. Is there anything else you can tell us, please?'

'No, I'm sorry, but that is all the information I have.'

The mayor continued, 'May I provide you both with some refreshment?'

The sergeant replied, 'No, thank you, we haven't the time. Thank you for what you have told us. We must leave you and report back immediately. We need your fastest horses. Princess Scarlett wants this information as soon as possible.'

The mayor turned to Sergeant Clough. 'Sergeant, see to these people immediately. Give them fresh horses and anything else they need.' He turned back. 'Farewell, we may meet again at the coronation.'

Sergeant Wilbur bowed to the mayor. 'It would be a pleasure.' Sergeant Clough led the messengers out.

The mayor then went to the anteroom where Sir Philip had been listening to what had taken place. The mayor gave out a great sigh, sat and wiped his brow. 'That had me worried for a minute. Princess Scarlett must be getting worried. She needs the Great Ring of Falconia for her coronation. It's supposed to be very magical for its rightful owner who is supposed to be the ruler of Falconia.'

'I'll be glad when this is all over and we've finally gotten rid of Princess Scarlett,' Sir Philip replied.

'So will just about everyone else in the kingdom,' the mayor answered.

The next morning the castle once again was a hive of activity. It was the eve of the coronation and the excitement, even for an evil princess, was palpable. More people were arriving at the castle and the town was almost bursting at the seams. The Throne Room was now decorated with flowers everywhere. Guests mingled with the servants, who were making the final touches to the room. Chairs were being placed all around the room and people with lists were placing name cards on the chairs and then changing some of them as some of the guests that were present complained about being too far away. Some were changed if it was thought that the complaint was warranted. Some complaints resulted in the complainant being moved further away or even out of the Throne Room altogether. Princess Scarlett sat on the queen's throne watching the activity with a very bored expression.

From amongst the chaos, the Captain of the Guard appeared. Princess Scarlett saw him and shouted, 'Stop! Everybody out and secure the doors. Now!'

One of the supervisors turned, and said, 'But we have no time to stop. This work must be done.'

The princess screamed, 'What!' and pointed her finger

at him. He started to choke. His hands went to his throat and he fell to his knees. Then he started to turn blue and writhed frantically on the floor. Shortly he was dead. 'Is anyone else here going to question my commands?' No one even dared to speak. They were all heading as fast as they could out of the Throne Room. Only the Captain of the Guard did not leave but bowed to the princess who asked him, 'What news do you have for me?'

The captain said, 'Two of your messengers have returned from Thomastown with the information that the five creatures had been there. They then headed towards the forest in pursuit of Sir Philip and his companions. This has been confirmed by another messenger who found a forester who had seen the monsters entering the forest.'

The princess frowned. When she had almost killed Charlotte in her dreams, the group had been on the edge of the forest not far from Thomastown. She had thought they would have headed for Thomastown with the injured Charlotte rather than back into the forest. 'Send another messenger to actually find the creatures. Tell them that it is urgent they find the fake Great Ring of Falconia one of the fugitives is carrying and get the one with the crow's wings, Dilly or Dally, or whatever its name is, to fly it here at once. Quick, do it now and send me the Royal Chamberlain.' The captain bowed and left.

The Royal Chamberlain entered and bowed. The princess asked him, 'Is the mayor of Thomastown coming to my coronation?'

The Royal Chamberlain answered, 'Of course, Your Majesty.'

'Is he here yet?' Princess Scarlett asked.

The Royal Chamberlain answered, 'I will find out at once. Please excuse me and I will find out at once.' He repeated himself nervously, bowed once again and started to turn to leave.

Princess Scarlett halted him with a wave of her hand. 'See that he is summoned to me at once, or as soon as he arrives. Oh, and get that body out of here. It may upset my guests.' The princess went back and sat on the Throne as the organisers and workers cautiously re-entered the Throne Room.

CHAPTER 32

Mayor Reading, Healer Woodcraft, Charlotte, Sir Philip, Burger Rowles, Gerry, several other Thomastown councillors, Sergeant Clough and a dozen town guards prepared to leave Thomastown early the next morning to be the delegation from Thomastown, to the coronation. Charlotte and Sir Philip were heavily disguised, especially Charlotte because, whereas there were only a few guards who would recognise Sir Philip, everyone would recognise Charlotte. As Sir Philip was saddling Jenny, she gave him a strange look, as if saying, 'Who are you?' Sir Philip whispered in her ear, 'It's really me, honest.' Jenny gave a shake of her head and stood patiently to be saddled.

As they were leaving, Mayor Reading told the others

that they should arrive at Falconia Castle in the middle of that afternoon for the noon coronation the day after, Princess Charlotte's and Princess Scarlett's sixteenth birthday. The trip was uneventful and they entered the town unchallenged, just one of many groups entering the town of Falconia for the coronation. The town was a mass of people and the mayor led his group very slowly through the throng so as not to injure anyone in the crowd. There were decorations everywhere and almost every building showed at least one blue and green banner with the Falcon of Falconia holding the Great Ring in its claws.

They finally got to the castle gate which was guarded. Mayor Reading announced that they were the delegation from Thomastown. The guards conferred with each other and told them to wait while the Captain of the Guards was summoned. When the captain came, he had two dozen armed guards with him. Together with the Gate Guards, there were over thirty soldiers. He went up to Mayor Reading and ordered him to come with him while the others waited at the gate. The captain and the mayor left with two soldiers, leaving the rest of the troops watching the remaining delegation at the gate. Sir Philip casually sauntered over to Sergeant Clough, and whispered, 'We might have to fight our way out of this.'

The sergeant, looking around, answered also in a whisper, 'I hope not because we'll lose, but don't worry, the mayor is a fast thinker and talker. He'll get us out of it.'

Sir Philip, also looking round, answered, 'I hope you're right.'

As the mayor was being led to the Throne Room, Captain Miland told him, 'Don't forget to call Princess Scarlett Your Majesty, not Your Highness.' The mayor nodded. Mayor Reading was led into the well-decorated Throne Room where servants were still working getting more ready for the coronation and some guests were checking to see where they were seated. The guards led him up the central aisle to the front of the podium where the princess was sitting on the throne. The mayor bowed. 'I am honoured to meet you, Your Majesty, may your reign be long and prosperous.'

Princess Scarlett stood and smiled. 'Thank you for your sentiments. They are well appreciated.' Princess Scarlett continued in a louder voice, 'All of you leave.' This time no one spoke. There was just a mad scramble for the doors.

When the only people in the room were the princess, Mayor Reading and the captain — the two guards also had been ordered to leave — the princess spoke. 'I am glad you are here. I believe you have a VIP seat close to the front, isn't that right?' she asked Captain Miland. The captain answered with a stutter, 'I er … I don't know. I um … er … will check the lists.'

Princess Scarlett rolled her eyes. 'If he hasn't, make sure he gets one.' She turned back to the mayor, 'I believe you met with some strange creatures two days ago.'

The mayor nodded. 'Yes, Your Majesty.'

'The princess asked, 'What did they say?'

The mayor answered, 'The one with the lion's head asked about some enemies of Falconia that you were after, several men and a girl. We spoke over the town wall. We were rather concerned about what may happen if we let them in.'

'That is understandable. What did you tell them?' the princess asked.

The mayor furrowed his brow in thought. 'Only that we hadn't seen the group they were after, but if we did, we would apprehend them immediately and send messengers both to you and them, letting you and them know we had caught them. I must admit I did ask if there was a reward.'

The princess laughed. 'And what did they say?'

The mayor reddened. 'The lion-headed one said that serving Princess Scarlett of Falconia was reward enough. They then headed towards the forest and that was the last I saw of them.'

The princess laughed again. 'Thank you for your information. You may now leave and bring your delegation into the castle. I hope you and your friends and comrades have a good time tomorrow.' She called back the guards.

The mayor bowed, and said, 'Thank you, Your Majesty,' then turned to leave. The doors to the Throne Room opened and the two guards came in to escort the mayor back to the gate.

As the mayor left, the princess whispered to Captain Miland, 'Captain, put an extra watcher on that group.'

The captain bowed. 'Yes, Your Majesty.'

The mayor returned to his delegation. They were then led by two guards to the mayor's friend's house. The friend, Sir George Potts, the Royal Falconer, the man responsible for Falconia's internal security, had a sizeable residence inside the main keep of the castle. The mayor and Healer

Woodcraft were given a room to share; Charlotte was given her own room; and Sir Philip, Burger Rowles, Sergeant Clough and Gerry shared a room. The other councillors shared a dormitory and the guards shared with the horses in the stables and stable yard. They also helped keep watch.

Later that day in the house's dark walnut-panelled dining room, which had a table that was large enough for over twenty diners, Sir George, dressed in his customary green and brown, presided over a sumptuous dinner which was attended by Charlotte, Sir Philip, Mayor Reading, Healer Woodcraft, Burger Rowles, Sergeant Clough and Fabian Hastings, Sir George's head of security.

Sergeant Clough gave a loud belch. 'That was by far the best meal I've ever eaten.'

Sir George smiled. 'I'm glad you enjoyed it.' During the meal, Sir George and Fabian Hastings had been told all about what had happened to Charlotte from the time of the harpy attack to their arrival at Falconia. Sir Philip left out the story of his journey from Falconia to Harbourtown and Sir George already knew that there had been an incident between Sir Philip and Princess Scarlett, but not the complete details. Sir Philip enlightened him. Now the meal was over, Sir George said, 'Well, that explains some of the strange events that took place at your birth,

Princess Charlotte.'

Charlotte looked at him. 'What were they?'

Sir George rested his chin on his hands for a few moments, then started his story. 'When your father died about two months before you were born that broken medallion around your neck was around his, except it was whole. It disappeared when he died, and no one knew what had happened to it.'

Charlotte interrupted. 'How did he die?'

Sir George shook his head. 'Good question, he just suddenly became sick and two weeks later he was dead. He had a very learned nurse who looked after him and she was devastated when he died. It was rumoured at the time that she also knew a little magic.' Sir George paused, while thinking. 'Moving on to your actual birth. Queen Katerina was extremely large during her pregnancy and we were all incredibly surprised when a tiny Princess Scarlett appeared a week later.'

Sir Philip interrupted. 'Er ... didn't you notice her twin?'

Sir George shook his head. 'No, no one ever saw the twin — I mean you.' He shook his head again, looking at Charlotte. 'Please, no more interruptions until I have finished. For several days before the birth and a week-and-a-half after, no one was allowed into the queen's chambers except for three people. A doctor supplied by the Duchess of Mayflor, a wet nurse supplied by the Duchess of Mayflor, and someone who should have been a midwife supplied by the Duchess of Mayflor, except that just before your birth the midwife somehow fell into the moat. There was not much left of her. A midwife was needed urgently and the best we had was your father's nurse, who was sworn to secrecy before being allowed to assist. I am only guessing now, but when you and your sister were born, somehow, she managed to give you both half of that medallion and then Dobbin took you away from Falconia never to be seen again, until today. It was a bad time for midwives just then in Falconia, as the king's nurse conveniently fell down some stairs and broke her neck shortly after the birth. The doctor and wet nurse went back to Mayflor when Princess Scarlett got older.'

There was silence for a few moments. Sir Philip asked, 'Wouldn't anyone from Falconia have noticed Charlotte in Harbourtown and noticed that she looked like Princess Scarlett?'

'Very few people from Falconia would have cause to go to Harbourtown. You would have to travel all the way around the Great Forest to get there. Our trade goes to or through Thrackstown and the Seven Duchies.' Sir George frowned. 'I must admit we do receive letters from a contact in Harbourtown, but he is a native of Harbourtown and has never been to Falconia.'

Charlotte looked shocked. 'Who is it?'

Sir George answered, with a smile, 'If you become queen, I will tell you.'

'You wouldn't have anyone like that in Concordia, though, would you?' Sir Philip enquired.

Sir George didn't answer, but just smiled.

Sir Philip, slightly taken aback, then asked, 'Why didn't you become king on the death of your nephew?'

Sir George answered, sadly, 'I did have two sons, but they both were killed at the Battle of Duchies Pass. The queen was pregnant with what looked like would be a strapping boy. I decided to let the queen take the throne, expecting it would pass down to her son. Instead, we got Princess Scarlett.' He shook his head. 'And tomorrow she will be queen unless we can stop her. I suggest you all go to bed as we will have a long, dangerous day tomorrow. Fabian and I will work on a plan and we will discuss it with you all early tomorrow, but first, everyone stand and toast the gracious lady, who will be the new Queen of Falconia.' He nodded towards Charlotte. 'I will be the first to announce a toast to who will be the next Queen of Falconia. I give you Queen Charlotte.' They all raised their glasses and toasted Charlotte. Charlotte blushed and nodded her thanks. Sir George continued, 'And now I wish you all goodnight.'

The others all wished Sir George and Fabian goodnight and went to bed. No one had a good night's sleep.

Princess Scarlett went to her rooms expecting to have to kill the third maid. She had just about given up on her hope to find the medallion before the coronation. She didn't mind too much. Her half wouldn't help her sister as she must either be dead or many miles away. She just hoped she would get confirmation soon. The Great Ring of Falconia was another matter. She hoped she could get away with the fake for the coronation if she was forced to. She didn't really want it to come to that though. After tomorrow, it would all be different. She would be stronger after tomorrow, her sixteenth birthday. Also, she would be queen. Her birthday and the fact she would be queen would increase her powers and soon, whatever happened, she would be the true owner of the Great Ring of Falconia, the power there was phenomenal.

Princess Scarlett entered her rooms. The guards all stood at attention. The maid was nowhere to be seen. It would not take long to find her.

CHAPTER 33

Finally, it had arrived, Charlotte's birthday. It was also Princess Scarlett's birthday and the day of the coronation. The atmosphere around the castle was so tense you could have cut it with a knife. Everyone in the castle who was working was having a quick, early breakfast; even Princess Scarlett didn't sleep in. Sir John Amberleigh, the Royal Chamberlain, seemed to be in half a dozen places at once, trying to make sure everything was going smoothly. He was doing a good job, making sure all the last-minute problems disappeared. Princess Scarlett was with her new maids getting ready for the coronation in the best guest suite. Her "friends" had all stopped by to wish her luck and the princess had thanked them and told them to go and find their seats.

She was not supposed to enter the Throne Room until the ceremony. She had left orders that she was to be informed immediately, even if the ceremony had begun, the moment Dolly the flying creature landed. When her new maids had finished getting her dressed, she looked resplendent. Her long, blonde tresses were tied up in a bun. Her dress was jet black and, for her, particularly modest. It was suggested to her that she wear a white dress, but she refused. She wore a ruby choker, the colour of blood. There were rubies and diamonds sewn around her dress and she wore strong, black, leather ankle boots. She also had a black fur cloak with grey ermine edges. Everyone who saw her had to admit she looked stunning. She sat waiting to be told it was time to go to the Throne Room. She also waited for news.

At the Royal Falconer's house, everything was also in a turmoil. The mayor had been informed that he and Healer Woodcraft would be in the third row in the Throne Room. Everyone else would either be in the Keep Courtyard or in the market square, which had been cleared of tents and traders, waiting for the new queen to make an appearance. Sir George Potts, the Royal Falconer, was heading a meeting in his study. At the meeting were himself, Mayor Reading, Healer Woodcraft, Charlotte, Sir Philip, Burger Rowles, Gerry, Sergeant Clough, Fabian Hastings and another of the Royal Falconer's assistants, a tall, dark-haired, burly man called William.

Sir George Potts got up to speak. 'Before we start, I want to wish Princess Charlotte a happy and memorable birthday. Whatever happens, I'm sure it will be a day she never forgets.' He paused while everyone at the table wished Charlotte a happy birthday, then continued. 'I, Mayor Reading and Healer Woodcraft all have to be in the Throne Room for the coronation ceremony. There are quite a few people who will be in there who hated the old queen and hate Princess Scarlett. Some are ready to make the move to rebel if and when a definite signal is given. Fabian and his assistant, William' — Fabian and William nodded acknowledgements — 'will smuggle Sir Philip, Charlotte, Sergeant Clough and two of his men into the castle. They will go in via the old Falconers' Gate at the back of the castle, which has hardly been used since King Edmond mysteriously died. There will be no guards there; we have been fortunate that most of the castle guards have left the castle in order to help protect the mines from the dwarfs.'

Charlotte asked, 'What are the dwarfs doing?'

Sir George answered, 'They are trying to take over the mines. That will be one of the first things you will have to deal with should you, er … my apologies, Your Highness, I mean, when you become queen.' He continued, 'Burger Rowles will join half the real councillors, the other half have been replaced by Townsville guards, and be in the Keep Courtyard as will some of my most trusted men. Gerry, the rest of the guards and some more of my men will be in the marketplace. Remember, you have allies who will definitely fight to get rid of Princess Scarlett and there are many others who will join in if it looks like we can win.'

Charlotte then addressed the room, while lifting her medallion so that everybody could see it. 'We will look for the other half of this medallion. I have been told that putting the two halves together will solve our problems. What will happen' — she shrugged — 'I don't know.' She took the purple crystal from her pouch and held it up. 'This has been glowing stronger since I entered the castle. It will lead us to the other half.'

The Royal Falconer said, 'I hope you are right. Princess Scarlett has been tearing her rooms apart without success looking for the other half of that medallion. She has already murdered three of her maids for failing to find it, so it must be important. I hope you're right about that crystal.'

Charlotte gripped the crystal. 'I'm sure I am. Colin's crystals have always worked well in the past.'

It was Sir Philip's turn to speak. 'The sergeant, his men and your men' — he pointed to Fabian and William both wearing the blue and green livery of Falconia — 'and myself are to protect Princess Charlotte until she finds the other half of the medallion and then get her back to the Throne Room.' He smiled. 'Easy.'

Sergeant Clough now had a turn, while looking grim. 'This house was watched last night. Nothing much happened. The watch was changed at eight o'clock about fifteen minutes ago. Unfortunately, the new watcher was mugged by early rising criminals. He is not likely to survive.'

Burger Rowles looked shocked, and asked, 'Was that a good idea? Won't he be missed?'

The sergeant replied, 'In four hours we will either have won, be dead, or wish we were dead. I don't think his demise matters, or that he will even be missed, until this is all over.'

The Royal Falconer said, 'We have to be in our places in the Throne Room by ten o'clock. All our other people will be in place at about the same time. At eleven-thirty Princess Charlotte and the others will enter the castle via the Falconers' Gate, and don't forget Princess Charlotte has the real Great Ring of Falconia. The one in the Throne Room is a fake. Good luck.'

They all left the room to go to prepare for their tasks.

At eleven-thirty, Princess Scarlett went to the rear entrance to the dais in the Throne Room ready to enter it and take the crown. Daisy had still not arrived. She was incredibly nervous because the ceremony was partially magical, and she should have had the Great Ring of Falconia in there. She hoped the fake ring would be adequate.

Charlotte was also feeling anxious. She — this time without a disguise as it was thought she may need to show herself as the twin to Princess Scarlett — and the others were making their way through the Falconers' Gate at the back of the castle. Charlotte was wearing the real Great Ring of Falconia. The purple crystal was glowing brighter with every step. She hoped that she would find the other half of the medallion before the ceremony was over, but had no idea what would happen when she did. They entered the castle with deep foreboding.

CHAPTER 34

Sir George Potts, Mayor Reading and Healer Woodcroft had taken their appointed places in the Throne Room. Sir George was in the front row, while the mayor and Healer Woodcroft were in the third row. They had been honoured with their positions as no other mayor and assistant were closer than the fifth row. They didn't know that the men sitting on either side of them were guards in disguise. The Throne Room was looking resplendent with flowers and other decorations everywhere. The doors to the balcony were open so that the people in the courtyard could at least hear the ceremony even though they couldn't see it. The people were also colourful with representatives from all the towns in Falconia and from the major guilds and merchant organisations. There were also representatives from the Seven Duchies, Melita and Thrackstown. Harbourtown and Concordia didn't have representatives as these two places weren't able to have anyone there in time. There were guards in the Throne Room, but not many — two by the doors and a pair on either side of the dais. Trouble was not expected, at least by the organisers.

The men accompanying Charlotte and Sir Philip had been warned that they may receive help from a wolf and/or an eagle while in the castle. The men, knowing that strange and magical occurrences happened around members of the Falconia family, made no comment.

When Charlotte and the others entered the castle through the Falconers' Gate, the Royal Falconer's assistants started to lead the group towards Princess Scarlett's rooms. Charlotte, with the purple crystal in her hand, watched it fade slightly and so called a halt. 'That's the wrong way. It's this way.' She set off in the opposite direction. Fabian whispered to her, 'But Princess Scarlett's rooms are this way,' and pointed.

Charlotte shook her head and answered, 'The crystal says this way and I trust the crystal.'

Fabian shrugged. 'You're in charge,' and everyone followed her down the corridor. It was twenty minutes before twelve o'clock.

They rounded a corner and right in front of them was a half-helmed, mail-clad guard with a halberd. The guard looked at Charlotte in amazement and then bowed. 'Your Majesty, I thought you were in the Throne Room's anteroom.'

Charlotte answered, attempting the most authoritative voice she could, 'Well, obviously I'm not. Continue with your duties.' The guard stood at attention and watched the seven people pass him and continue down the corridor. He wondered why Princess Scarlett wasn't wearing the clothes he had seen her in earlier for the coronation. He decided that there could be something wrong and should go looking for his sergeant and report his sighting. He found his sergeant, Sergeant Ratch, with half a dozen guards and told him what had happened. The sergeant agreed that what the guard had seen was strange and ordered the guard to go and report what he had seen to Captain Miland. He ordered the rest of his men to follow him to search for the intruders and find out what was happening.

Charlotte and the rest of her party were moving slowly, watching the crystal's brightness slowly increase in intensity. This meant that it didn't take long for the sergeant and his guards to catch up with them. The sergeant shouted at them to stop and when they didn't, he sent one of his men to call for more guards. Sergeant Clough said to Charlotte, 'Keep going as fast as you can and find the medallion. Sir Philip and Fabian go with her. The rest of you with me.'

Sergeant Clough, his two men from Thomastown, and William, the Royal Falconer's man, all of them armed only with swords, spread across the corridor to stop the guards getting past them to Charlotte. The castle sergeant and five guards armed with halberds advanced slowly and cautiously towards them.

Just outside the Throne Room, the Captain of the Guard, Gill Miland, had received the guard's report and so knocked and entered the anteroom. Princess Scarlett looked at him with delight. 'The cow has finally arrived?'

'Not yet, Your Majesty, I have other news,' Captain Miland told her.

'It had better be important!' Princess Scarlett glared at the captain.

'A guard has reported that someone that looks like

you, together with six men, have entered the castle and now are heading towards the western part of the castle,' Captain Miland informed the princess.

Princess Scarlett's brow wrinkled with thought. 'But that's away from my rooms.' A look of realisation came upon her, and she screamed, 'The nursery! Of course, the nursery. Send every man you can find to stop this imposter reaching it. NOW!' Captain Miland rushed from the room.

Princess Scarlett stormed into the Throne Room causing everyone to stop talking and look up at her, then start talking in asides. She strode to the centre of the dais and glared at the Royal Chamberlain, dressed in the fur-lined ceremonial robes and gold chain of his office. 'Start the ceremony and hurry it up. NOW!' She stomped to the Throne and sat and glowered at the assembled throng which, after a few murmurs, went quiet under her glare.

The Royal Chamberlain thought about mentioning that it was still only ten minutes to twelve, but prudently decided against it. Princess Scarlett sat on the Throne as he walked to the plinth where the symbols of Falconia rested. He picked up the royal orb and raised it over his head to present it to the assembled citizens and dignitaries. He then turned and held it out to the Princess,

'Do you take this, the Great Orb of Falconia and promise to use it for the prosperity of the people of Falconia?'

Princess Scarlett nodded solemnly and said in a loud voice, 'I, Princess Scarlett take the Great Orb of Falconia and promise to use it for the prosperity of the people of Falconia.' Sir John presented it to her, and she took it, placing it in the crook of her left arm.

Sir John then picked up the sceptre. He raised it over his head to present it to the citizens present in the Throne Room. He then turned and held it out to the princess. 'Do you take this, the Great Sceptre of Falconia and promise to use it for the protection of the people of Falconia?'

Princess Scarlett, who was getting impatient, once again nodded solemnly. She said loudly, 'I, Princess Scarlett, take the Great Sceptre of Falconia and promise to use it for the protection of the people of Falconia.' She added with a whisper, 'Hurry it up, you fool. I want this finished.' Sir John presented the princess with the sceptre, which was rested on her right leg and supported by her right arm.

Sir John, visibly shaken, went back to the plinth and picked up the crown. This time he didn't present it to the crowd, but went straight back to the princess and babbled quickly, 'Do you take this, the Great Crown of Falconia and promise to use it to rule fairly for all the people of Falconia?'

'I promise, now get on with it,' Princess Scarlett snapped at the Royal Chamberlain. The crowd began to murmur at this, but both Sir John and the princess ignored them as the crown was placed carefully on her head.

It was now the turn of the Great Ring of Falconia. The Royal Chamberlain went to the plinth and took the ring. This time he did raise it above his head in presentation to those assembled and turned back to Princess Scarlett. Sir John intoned quickly, 'Do you take this, the Great Ring of Falconia and promise to use it for the benefit and greatness of the Kingdom of Falconia?'

This was it. The big test. Princess Scarlett said in a much quieter voice and with a sense of foreboding, 'I, Princess Scarlett, take this, the Great Ring of Falconia and promise to use it for the benefit and greatness of the Kingdom of Falconia.'

Sir John then went to place the ring on the ring finger of her right hand. As it reached the top of her finger, there was a clap of thunder and the fake ring burst into flames. Sir John Amberleigh, his hands burning, screamed and threw the ring into the air where it hovered, still burning.

Princess Scarlett jumped up off the throne, dropping both the orb and the sceptre to the floor. There was uproar in the Throne Room with people jumping up and shouting and pointing at the hovering, burning ring. Some shouted, 'Fraud', 'Fake', 'Treason' and 'Imposter'. Princess Scarlett screamed with rage and pointed her finger at the shouting and confused crowd. A bolt of lightning flew from her fingertips and exploded killing several people instantly and wounding more. People started to dive for cover as Princess Scarlett sent another bolt of lightning into the crowd killing and wounding even more people. She then took the crown off her head and threw it angrily on the Throne and stormed out the back of the Throne Room to head towards the nursery.

Sergeant Clough and the other three were standing firm as the guards approached with their halberds lowered, easily outreaching their opponents' swords. The small group exchanged nervous glances as they knew they could not win this fight but only delay the guards. And then the screams started; not from the sergeant and his men, but from the guards who suddenly found a giant wolf amongst them. It bit out the throat of one of them and disembowelled another with its claw before they were able to react and, even then, they couldn't do much. Halberds are not very maneuverable in a corridor and

Jason brought down another guard by mauling his leg before the others dropped their weapons and started to run. Jason let them go and left the injured one cowering on the floor of the corridor. Sergeant Clough smiled at Jason, approached him and chuckled, 'Thanks, puppy.' Jason growled at him, but still allowed the sergeant to tickle him under the chin. The sergeant shook his head and looked back down the corridor where Charlotte and the others had gone. 'Charlotte, please hurry, we won't get away with that again.'

CHAPTER 35

When the fake Great Ring of Falconia burst into flames with the clap of thunder, it caused Charlotte and her companions to pause in their search. The real Great Ring of Falconia on Charlotte's finger glowed and became warm. Sir Philip whispered to Charlotte, 'What do you think that was?'

'I think that was the fake ring being destroyed. My ring definitely reacted when the thunder occurred.'

'That's the first time you've called the ring yours.' Sir Philip smiled at Charlotte. 'Is it much further?'

Charlotte looked at the purple crystal in her hand and answered, 'The glow is getting stronger, so we are getting closer.'

Sir Philip turned to Fabian and asked, 'What's down this way?'

Fabian answered, 'This is the way to the royal kitchens, the royal private dining room and the royal nursery.'

Charlotte eyes widened with surprise. 'The royal nursery; that must be it. I must have been born there, and so would have Scarlett. Could the medallion be there?' She turned back to the corridor while asking, 'Is it far?'

Fabian answered, 'No, we're almost there.' They continued down the corridor towards the nursery.

Princess Scarlett met Captain Miland just outside the anteroom of the Throne Room. He was with a squad of a dozen men plus the two guards who had been sent back by Sergeant Ratch. 'I told you to send all the guards to the nursery,' she snapped.

'I have sent a squad already. When they meet up with Sergeant Ratch and his men, they will outnumber the intruders by almost three to one. I thought I should make sure you were safe,' the captain answered, nervously.

'I hope that will be enough. Follow me, we are going to the nursery.' The princess headed down the corridor at a brisk pace closely followed by her guards.

Back at the scene of the skirmish with the guards, the injured guard had passed out. Jason suddenly sniffed the air and bounded down the corridor following the direction that Charlotte and the others had gone, away from the direction where the guards had fled. Sergeant Clough shouted to the others, 'After him. He'll be heading for Charlotte.' They all ran after the wolf.

In the Throne Room, people were picking themselves up, some were helping the more badly wounded, which included the guard who had been sitting next to Healer Woodcroft. The healer was fumbling in his pouch for medications to help the guard.

There were murmurings everywhere and shouts of anger against Princess Scarlett. Her supporters had the good sense to remain quiet. The two guards by the doors had left to find help for the injured, while the other four stood with their halberds horizontal in front of the dais to prevent anyone climbing onto it. Sir George Potts, who had been in the front row for the ceremony due to his rank, pushed past them and jumped up on the dais and raised his hand for silence. He spoke in a very low, loud voice. 'We have seen what Princess Scarlett really thinks of us, but she is a fake. The real and true heir to the Throne of Falconia is her twin sister, the Princess Charlotte.' Most of the people in the Throne Room looked at each other in confusion. He raised his voice. 'She is here, now. We must raise her to the Throne before the fake Princess Scarlett can stop her. Who's with me?' The stunned crowd was silent. Sir George started chanting, 'Charlotte, not Scarlett.' Then Mayor Reading and some of Sir George's confidants, who knew something may happen, joined in. 'Charlotte, not Scarlett.' Sir George punched the air with his hook as he chanted.

The disguised guard who was next to Mayor Reading started to shout at Sir George, 'Stop! This is treason. The Princess Scarlett is now our queen.'

This angered several of the survivors near him who, along with the mayor, set upon him and soon he was unconscious. While this happened, more people in the crowd started chanting, and then not just them but most of the survivors of Princess Scarlett's attack also took it up. The crowd surged forward past the guards, who dropped their halberds and left the hall rather than fight against impossible odds. The crowd then climbed onto the dais and started moving towards the door that Princess Scarlett had left by, chanting as they went, 'Charlotte, not Scarlett.' Soon the only people who were left in the

Throne Room were the dead, the wounded, their helpers, most of the women and those who for various reasons either supported Princess Scarlett or wished to remain neutral, such as the various ambassadors.

In the Keep Courtyard, the crowd of about four to five hundred people were the more prosperous citizens of Falconia whose status had got them into the castle but not the Throne Room. They were mainly merchants and minor members of court or the delegations of the towns. This included some of the various town guards that had been brought with the delegations. They all made a colourful sight. They had heard the clap of thunder and the two explosions through the open doors on the balcony but didn't know what they signified. People were milling around confused and surprised. Then they heard the chanting. Burger Rowles ordered the others that were with him from Thomastown to take up the chant immediately. 'Charlotte, not Scarlett.'

Some of the various towns' officials had previously been warned that something may happen by the messages sent out by both Sir George and Mayor Reading. These and the guards that were with them also took up the chant. The merchants of Falconia had been suppressed and heavily taxed for years. Any protest from them resulting in an interview with the moat monsters, so even though most still had no idea what was going on, they joined the chant.

One of Mayor Reading's senior assistants drew his sword, and shouted, 'To the Throne Room.' Burger Rowles immediately drew his also. The guards from Thomastown did the same except for one who went down to the marketplace to inform Gerry what was happening. Members of the crowd followed Burger Rowles and took up his cry and surged towards the Keep Courtyard's main castle entrance, still not knowing what was happening. The guards at the main entrance crossed their halberds to stop the crowd and other guards presented their weapons point first at the crowd, resulting in the crowd halting.

Several of the crowd opened the closed West Gate into the castle. There were only two guards behind the door. One of the men shouted, 'This way! No Guards,' even though there were two there. These were quickly disarmed and tied up. Most of the people in the Keep Square poured through the West Gate and found the stairs leading to the upper levels. They surged up the stairs, chanting as they went, 'Charlotte, not Scarlett.' The guards at the main entrance continued to guard it as they had been ordered.

In the market square was the biggest crowd. There were over eight hundred people consisting of the poorer people of Falconia. The poorer merchants, the general townsfolk and more than a few farmers — those who did not rate an invitation into the castle. They heard the clap of thunder out of a clear, blue sky and didn't understand it. They didn't hear the explosions or the chanting from the Throne Room, but they did the chanting from the Keep.

Gerry and the others with him were unsure of what was happening and therefore didn't know what to do. He went and asked one of the guards at the outer castle gate what was going on. The guard said he did not know but he and his squad looked incredibly nervous. Just then, the man whom Burger Rowles had sent exited the gate and went into conference with Gerry. Gerry went back to the men he was with and told them to follow his lead. He then took up the chant, 'Charlotte, not Scarlett,' followed by his co-conspirators.

The crowd in the marketplace looked around in bewilderment, confused about the events that were occurring. Gerry jumped up onto a pillar in the centre of the square and shouted, 'Princess Scarlett is a fraud. The real and true princess is now here. We want Queen Charlotte.' He, his men and Sir George's men resumed chanting, 'Charlotte, not Scarlett.' The crowd in the market square stood around in stunned silence, then some of them took up the chant. Most of the crowd were slow to take up the chant; perhaps it was because of the oppression they had been living under for sixteen years, but eventually they too joined in and the crowd moved towards the gate into the castle.

The guards who were protecting the gate from the marketplace into the castle proper lowered their halberds at the crowd and killed over a dozen people before they were trampled underfoot. This had the added effect of enraging the crowd. As the mob surged into the castle, other guards they came across either ran or surrendered.

On the way to the nursery, Princess Scarlett could not help but hear the chanting coming from the Throne Room. She snarled, 'I will make them all pay for this.' She turned to the captain. 'Leave some men here to stop that ridiculous mob and you and the rest of your men follow me.' The captain left ten men to defend the corridor and followed.

Chapter 36

The squad of men who had been ordered to the nursery met the survivors of the skirmish against Sergeant Clough and his men and Jason. The squad listened in amazement as Sergeant Ratch described the encounter. The squad leader told the sergeant that they had been ordered to join Sergeant Ratch and go to the royal nursery and capture or kill the intruders there. Sergeant Ratch didn't really want to go back and face Jason again, but an order was an order, so he led the men back down the corridor towards the nursery.

When they reached the site of the skirmish, the guard with the injured leg had lost consciousness. The sergeant ordered two of his men to help the injured guard get back for medical assistance and then continued after the intruders.

Before they had gotten much further, they came to an adjoining passage. Sergeant Ratch paused. There was loud chanting coming from down the adjoining corridor. Suddenly, from around a corner, the crowd from the castle courtyard appeared chanting, 'Charlotte, not Scarlett.' They saw the guards, and someone shouted, 'Get them. Protect Charlotte.' They surged forward towards the guards.

Sergeant Ratch ordered, 'Halberds at the ready,' and led his men down the passage against the crowd.

Sir George Potts and the dignitaries from the Throne Room had encountered the ten guards Captain Miland had left to stop them. They all had their halberds at the ready to stop Sir George and the others getting any further. Sir George spread his arms out at his sides to halt his followers. 'Stop, I will talk to them.'

He approached the guards alone, only stopping when the halberds were almost touching his chest. He looked them over and spoke in a quiet, but firm voice, 'Hello, Josh, hello, Nick, Robbie, Brian,' addressing the older guards. 'I helped train you, oh, and you, Paul, I didn't see you for a moment, you younger ones will probably know me only by reputation. Sixteen years ago, I could have become King of Falconia. I didn't because that wasn't the right and legal thing to do. I supported the rightful heir, Queen Katerina.' He paused for a second. 'Once again, I am supporting the rightful heir to the Throne of Falconia, Princess Charlotte, not Scarlett who is a fraud and a faker. The clap of thunder you heard was the Ring of Falconia rejecting her.' He raised his real arm and pointed at the ceiling, 'Even the Ring knows she is a fake. You have a decision to make.' He lowered his arm to point at the guards. 'Are you going to murder, yes murder, as you are defending a fraud, these citizens of Falconia' — he half turned to spread his arm to include the crowd behind him — 'most of whom you have known and befriended for years, or are you going to get out of our way so that we can put the rightful heir on the throne?'

There were several moments of silence and then the older guards started to raise their halberds and move to the sides of the corridor. The younger ones took their lead from the older and they too moved to the sides of the corridor.

Sir George nodded towards them. 'Thank you, you have done the right thing.' He and the others from the

Throne Room walked past the guards following the path Princess Scarlett had taken.

Princess Scarlett, Captain Miland and the four guards had reached the corridor where a battle was in progress between the guards and the crowd from the Keep. The guards having the better weapons, had caused many casualties, but they were badly outnumbered and were being pushed back. Princess Scarlett stood at the end of the corridor and raised her arms towards the melee. Lightning flashed from her fingertips and explosions rent holes in the fighting, killing and wounding both guards and their opponents without discrimination. The fighting paused and everyone looked back down the corridor at Princess Scarlett, who raised her arms again and two more flashes caused explosions amongst the combatants in the corridor. The combatants, who were now almost entirely the crowd from the Keep, had enough. They turned and ran back around the corner of the corridor trampling over anyone who was still behind them. Princess Scarlett turned to the captain and his men, who were standing in stunned silence. 'Well, that stopped them. Now, to the nursery.' She started to continue down the corridor but had to stop as no one else had moved. 'Well, come on! Now!' she shouted. The men followed.

Charlotte, Sir Phillip and Fabian had entered the nursery. It was a moderately-sized room for the castle. It had two cots and a large play area with lots of dolls and other toys. There was also a kitchen area and numerous cupboards. It was painted pink. There were three doors into the nursery. Sir Philip and Fabian both looked at Charlotte. 'Where do we start?' Sir Philip asked.

Charlotte looked at the purple crystal; it was glowing brightly. She moved around the room. First, she moved towards the cots. Nothing happened. She moved towards a large pile of dolls and toys lying in a corner, the crystal started to glow even brighter. Sir Philip and Fabian went to join her at the toy pile, and they all started to sort through them. Charlotte picked up a large, blonde, well-dressed doll with a ceramic head and the crystal shone even brighter. Charlotte smiled and her face looked radiant as she whispered to Sir Philip and Fabian, 'I think I've found it.' They both looked at her expectantly as she began to unscrew the head from the doll.

'Still playing with dolls, dear sister.' Princess Scarlett stood smiling at the door at the far end of the room. The captain and four men were behind her. 'Have you found my half of the medallion? Throw me the doll.' She extended her hand.

From the corridor behind her the chanting was getting louder. The captain motioned for two of his men to investigate, but when they returned to the corridor, they heard the chanting getting even closer and, inexplicably, they went in the wrong direction.

Back at the nursery, Charlotte, Sir Philip and Fabian had frozen. Princess Scarlett repeated, 'Throw me the doll and I may let you all live as pets. After all, you are my sister. Oh, and throw me the Ring of Falconia also.'

Charlotte didn't move. Princess Scarlett shouted, 'NOW! Hurry.'

Sir Philip suddenly thought that maybe Princess Scarlett wasn't as powerful against Charlotte as everyone thought. He shouted to Charlotte, 'Get the medallion. Fabian with me.'

Sir Philip and Fabian charged towards Princess Scarlett. Her guards moved forward to protect her.

Princess Scarlett just laughed and raised her hand. Lightning sprang from her fingertips towards Sir Philip and Fabian. Just as the lightning was about to hit them a ray of green light suddenly emanated from the Great Ring of Falconia on Charlotte's hand and intercepted the lightning. The resulting explosion blew both Sir Philip and Fabian off their feet, unconscious. The explosion also knocked out Princess Scarlett's guards. The only people still standing were Princess Scarlett, Charlotte and Captain Miland of the Guard.

Princess Scarlett looked around, amazed. 'Hmm, the ring does things I didn't expect, but I'm sure you haven't mastered it yet. Goodbye, sister.' Princess Scarlett aimed the fingertips of both of her hands at Charlotte.

Charlotte had stopped unscrewing the doll's head. She smashed it against the wall instead. The other half of the medallion fell to the floor. This had the result of distracting Princess Scarlett so that her hands were slightly off target. What made her off target even more was that she was hit in the side by a giant wolf. The lightning, instead of hitting Charlotte, singed Jason's back and blew a hole in the wall.

Charlotte bent down and picked up the other half of the medallion. She placed that half next to the half around her neck so that she had a half in each hand.

There was a blinding burst of light as the two halves fused together. A blinding ray of light then emanated from the centre of the medallion, which hit Princess Scarlett, who screamed as a multitude of rays of coloured light burst out of the top of her head and smashed into Charlotte's head. Charlotte screamed and collapsed to the floor. Princess Scarlett's body began to shrink rapidly. In a few seconds, all that was left of Princess Scarlett was a pile of clothing on the floor. Jason moved to stand guard over Charlotte, his back smoking.

Sergeant Clough and his men arrived at the nursery. He looked around at all the unconscious people on the floor, the pile of clothes, and the captain who was still standing in a complete state of shock. The sergeant shook the captain. 'What happened?'

The captain just shook his head. 'I don't know, I saw it, but I don't know.'

The sergeant pointed at the unconscious body of Charlotte with Jason standing over her. 'Is that Charlotte or Scarlett?'

'I don't know,' was all the captain managed to utter.

Sergeant Clough looked closer at Charlotte's unconscious body, saw the fused medallion in her hands, the clothing which was the same as Charlotte was wearing when they entered the castle but, more importantly, that she was wearing the Great Ring of Falconia, and even more importantly the fact that Jason was standing over her, guarding her. 'That's Charlotte. We won.'

The crowd from the Throne Room arrived at the nursery, the Royal Falconer leading it. He took in the scene at one glance and took Captain Miland's sword and asked him, 'Did you see what happened?'

The captain just stood there, staring. Sir George turned to the sergeant. 'Sergeant Clough take the captain to the dungeons. We will question him later.' The sergeant and two men left with the captain.

The Royal Falconer took charge and started giving orders. He arranged for the castle guards and the chief royal advisors to be disarmed, arrested and replaced with men he could trust. He sent messengers to the crowds outside telling them Princess Scarlett was dead and ordered that the Guards Barracks be converted into a hospital for the many injured. The dead were to be also taken to the barracks until they could be identified, and their bodies claimed. He also ordered that the Throne Room be cleaned up ready for a coronation. 'Don't arrest the Royal Chamberlain; he will be needed for that.'

Healer Woodcraft, under the watchful eye of Jason, was examining Charlotte, trying to revive her. The Royal

Falconer went up to him. 'Is that her?'

Healer Woodcraft replied, 'She has all the marks of the injuries that she had when she came to Thomastown.'

The Royal Falconer gave a great sigh of relief. 'We did it. We did it.'

EPILOGUE

Everyone in the nursery finally regained consciousness. Fortunately, none were badly injured although all had some cuts, bruises and burns. The Throne Room was cleaned up and Charlotte went to her coronation. Once again, John Amberleigh, the Royal Chamberlain, performed the ceremony. He did it very gingerly, having his hands bandaged from the burns the fake ring had given him. Then he got to the part where he asked Charlotte, 'Do you take this, the Great Ring of Falconia and promise to use it for the benefit and greatness of the Kingdom of Falconia?'

Charlotte answered, 'I, Princess Charlotte take this, the Great Ring of Falconia, and promise to use it for the benefit and greatness of the Kingdom of Falconia.' Sir

John then placed the ring on the ring finger of her right hand. Instead of bursting into flame, it burst into a flash of bright light which surrounded Charlotte like a halo.

Sir John Amberleigh then turned to the assemblage, held his arms wide and announced, 'People of Falconia, I give you your new sovereign, Queen Charlotte.'

There were loud cheers and clapping from everyone in the room, even the ones that had supported Princess Scarlett. The cheers from the Keep were even louder as many of the people from the marketplace had also crowded in there.

Queen Charlotte then got up from the Throne to loud cheers and clapping and, after a minute, Sir John called for silence. She addressed the crowd. 'I must thank you all for the support you have given me. I thank you for the sacrifice you have made in order for this positive outcome to take place. I will be a good queen to Falconia for, I hope, many years. Now, you must excuse me. I have had a most amazing and challenging day, but first I must speak to my other Falconians.'

Queen Charlotte got down from the dais and made her way to the balcony doors. It took her a while as everyone wanted to congratulate her. Eventually, she got there, and she went out on the balcony to loud cheers from the Keep below. She raised her hands for silence. It took several